Horses! Big brutes weighing  rolling eyes, metal-tipped fe loony nun who scared me t infants. That's horses.

So when Jamie invited me and Leo to go with him to The Curragh where his grandfather was buying horses, I was less than chuffed. Almost didn't go.

But I did and the upside was David, who's part Aborigine, and Frank, who's an auctioneer and treated me like a grown-up when we sparkled conversationally at my first dinner-party.

As the Mills & Boon book Tilly lent me advised: 'Play one off against the other.' Which I did – and which turned out to be a pretty dumb steer. In fact, it turned out to be one of the World's Worst Ideas.

How I redeemed myself is – honestly – well worth reading about. Just in case it ever happens to you …

Mary Arrigan

maeve and the long-arm folly

Illustrated by Terry Myler

THE CHILDREN'S PRESS

To
Marcella

First published 1999 by
The Children's Press
an imprint of Anvil Books
45 Palmerston Road, Dublin 6

2 4 6 5 3 1

© Text Mary Arrigan 1999
© Illustrations Terry Myler

ISBN 1 901737 20 9

Typeset by Computertype Limited
Printed by Colour Book Limited

Contents

1

Horse Country

It's amazing how a simple conversation can lead to big happenings. The sort of happenings that make you wake up at night long afterwards and hug your knees as you remember. This is how it began.

We were sitting in our special place under a laurel hedge – me, my young cousin Leo, and our friend Jamie. I was staying with Leo – his mother is my aunt Brid. Jamie was staying with his grandfather, Mr McLaren, who owns a big house and stables just across the fields from Leo's place. Leo is a skinny little kid who likes brain-stirring stuff like surfing the net for useless information and reading books about hairy spiders and frogs that spit in your face

Jamie lives in London, but comes to stay with his grandfather pretty often. He has a frightfully posh accent, but is a regular guy in spite of that. He'd grown rather dishy too since I'd met him first. At that time he'd worn side-splittingly funny fair-isle jumpers and old-man sensible shoes. Now he was into Timberland boots and trendy hair. He was telling us about a trip he was making with his grandfather the next day. Mr McLaren was spending a few days in County Kildare, buying horses. Jamie wanted Leo and me to go too.

'I'm not big into horses, really,' I said. Horses are fine to look at as they tootle about in their own patch behind a stout fence. But face on they're big brutes with rolling eyes, metal-tipped feet, and teeth like the loony nun who scared me to death in high infants. No thank you, horses were not on my list of great entertainment.

'Grandad is going to the horse sales in Goffs,' went on Jamie. 'We could just hang out. No horses, I promise.'

'Where would we be staying?' I asked. It's always important to know your territory in advance.

'That's the great thing,' continued Jamie, excitement beaming all over his face. 'If you and Leo come, Grandad says we can stay in the Montgomery's lodge.'

'The Montgomerys?' I asked.

'Grandad's friends,' said Jamie. 'Their old housekeeper is retired and she lives in the lodge. We can stay there with her, so we wouldn't be at the house at all.'

I gave him a squinty look. 'Because we wouldn't fit in, me and Leo?' I said.

'Oh, can it, Maeve!' cried Leo.

Jamie shook his head patiently. 'No. It's just that Grandad thought that it would be more fun for us – if you'll come, that is. Leo is definitely on, aren't you?'

Leo nodded. 'Sure thing.'

'So, what about it, Maeve?' went on Jamie.

I could see that he was pushing hard for me to come. But I'd just been reading an excellent Mills and Boon book that my friend Tilly had given me. In it, a woman played really hard to get and had several hunks chasing after her like mad. You learn a lot from good books.

I sniffed, with just a tad of superiority. 'Dunno,' I said. 'I think not, Jamie. I think I just want to stay here in the country and be creative. Maybe write some poems.' That sounded good. Put me apart from the riff-raff. My poems are pretty good. I know because I'd been reading stuff by other women poets – Elizabeth Barrett-Browning Sylvia Plath and Emily Dickinson. I realised mine was better and that I didn't need consumption or tight corsets to make me great.

Jamie and Leo knew about my poetry writing, so I thought I might as well capitalise on it. I waited for Jamie to beg as I looked poetically into the distance.

THE PLEADING LOVER

By Maeve Morris

My love wants me to go with him.
He says without me life is grim.
'Let's flee, my sweet,' he begged and craved.
'We'll go where streets are brightly paved,
Filled with charm and sweet allure,
And there's no smell of horse manure.'

I didn't hear Jamie begging. I swivelled round and waited. And waited.

'Did you hear me?' I asked. 'I said I didn't think I could go.'

Jamie shrugged. 'Fair enough,' he said. 'You're old enough to make decisions for yourself.' He got up and grinned at Leo. 'Looks like it's just you and me. Better go and tell Grandad. Come on. Cheers, Maeve.'

Hold on, I thought. This was not supposed to turn out like this. Where were the pleading words: *Can't do without you, Maeve? No fun unless you're there too, Maeve?*

Leo jumped up and followed Jamie. I watched the two of them cross the lawn towards the french window of Mr McLaren's drawing-room. I had goofed. Abandoned here while those two went on a boys-only trip? No way!

'Wait!' I cried, dashing after them. 'I'll come.'

When I caught up with them in the drawing-room, they were both guffawing loudly. They'd been winding me up, the pair of them. I spluttered with anger.

'Called your bluff, mighty Maeve,' laughed Leo. 'We knew you'd hot-foot it after us, didn't we, Jamie?'

Jamie gave me a sheepish grin.

'Prats,' I hissed. But I didn't make any more threats.

'Very flat,' I said, as we drove across the Curragh.

'I know the story about the Curragh,' announced Leo. 'Saint Brigid wanted a small bit of land to build a convent on, so she went to the Governor, but he told her to go away. Saint Brigid kept on pleading with him so, eventually, just to get rid of her, he told her she could have as much land as her green cloak would cover...'

'Don't tell me,' I laughed. 'She knitted a parish ...'

Jamie turned around to face me. 'Let him tell his story, Maeve,' he said. 'Go on, Leo.'

Leo gave me a triumphant look before continuing. 'She spread out her green cloak,' he went on, 'and, to the amazement of everyone, it kept on spreading until it had covered the whole Curragh. Then she was able to build her monastery in Kildare, because the Governor had to keep to his word.'

'Good job she hadn't been wearing a tartan cloak, Leo,' I said. 'Or one with pink polka dots.'

'Nice story that, Leo,' said Mr McLaren. I could see him smiling in the driving-mirror and wished he'd smile at me like that.

After a while we came to big gates with the words Briarstown Stud forming a wrought-iron arch over them.

'Here we are,' said Mr McLaren. He spoke into one of those grill things you see on movie stars' gateways. With a quiet hiss, the gates swung open. A woman came out of the lodge and beamed at us. Her grey hair was tied back with a red ribbon and she was wearing baggy cords, boots, and a floppy sweater which indicated a naff branch of Oxfam around these parts. She had good-humoured eyes which crinkled as she laughed and waved at us. Jamie jumped out of the car and gave her a hug.

'Mrs O'Dea!' he exclaimed. He turned towards Leo and me. 'Mrs O'Dea has been here at Briarstown since forever,' he laughed.

'Know this lad since he was a bitty thing,' she said, holding out a plump hand to Leo and me. 'How d'ye do. Come in and make yourselves at home. I was delighted when Jamie rang last night and said you'd all be here in the lodge and not up in that draughty old house.'

Mr McLaren fished our bags out of the boot and, with a nod and a 'Cheerio', cruised up the avenue. The three of us followed Mrs O'Dea into the lodge. The tiny hall opened into an open-plan sitting-room and kitchen which were very modern for such an old place. There was lots of pine. The dresser didn't have the usual boring old willow-pattern stuff. Instead there were studio-type plates and mugs in really mad colours. The blinds on the diamond-paned windows were lime green. A basket of dried flowers stood in a small niche. The kitchen table was pine with ceramic tiles set into it. An old clock with those numbers that you can't read – don't know why they're called Roman numerals because I'm sure the Ancient Romans didn't have clocks – ticked loudly from the chimney breast. Two easy chairs and a small sofa with lime green throws were arranged around the red Stanley range. I knew it was a Stanley because Aunt Brid has one.

'Cosy,' I said. 'This is the sort of kitchen I'd like to have. Old fashioned with bursts of loud colours. Dead cool.'

Mrs O'Dea laughed. 'Not too cool, I hope. With the summers we get I like to keep the Stanley humming.

Come on, I'll show you to your rooms. You boys can have the back bedroom. Missy here will have the attic.'

As I followed her up the narrow stairs, I couldn't help wondering if the attic meant some grotty dump full of junk with an iron bedstead passing for comfort. I should have known better. The slanted ceiling and walls were painted sunshine yellow. The bed was covered with the sort of lacy duvet that you see in glossy mags. A white carpet boded well for my dainty toes, and the pretty bedside lamp boded well for writing midnight poems. A bowl of purple pot-pourri sent out a sweet aroma from the sunny window-sill. This was a cosy haven to inspire great ideas. If Sylvia Plath had had a place like this she'd never have done herself in.

'Brilliant!' I said again.

'Glad you like it. Now you get unpacked. Supper in half an hour. Do you like Indian curry?'

'You bet your boots I do,' I beamed. Life was distinctly looking rosy. Grand room, comfy house and a motherly old bird to fuss over me and cook good nosh. All this and Jamie too. Be still my beating heart!

The curry was a roaring volcano. In fact it made my eyes water and pray that I'd still have a roof on my mouth when the sizzling would die down. However I didn't splutter or scream, I simply drank water and smiled with poetic dignity and all that, though mainly because my teeth were welded together. The ice-cream and strawberries for afters undid some of the damage to my palate, but I crossed India off my list of places to visit.

Mrs O'Dea and Jamie spent a lot of time catching up on chat about people Leo and I had never heard of. I caught Leo's eye and made an exaggerrated yawning gesture and crossed my eyes. Mrs O'Dea caught us sniggering.

'Listen,' she said, ignoring our red faces, 'you must

meet David. He's staying with his mother just down the road. They've rented a cottage for the summer. He's much the same age as yourselves – thirteen or so.'

My ears pricked up. A David with the same number of years as myself sounded okay by me.

'Who is he?' asked Jamie.

He's competition for you, matey, I thought. Now I could do my Mills and Boon bit and juggle this David and Jamie. The words fatal dame, or something, came to mind.

'He's part Aborigine,' said Mrs O'Dea.

'He's what?' I asked.

'Part Aborigine,' put in Leo. 'Native Australians ...'

'I know who the Aborigines are,' I retorted. 'What's he doing here?' Why on earth would an Aborigine – even a part Aborigine – come to a soggy place like Ireland?'

'Well, if figures,' said Mrs O'Dea. 'People with any Irish blood in their veins like to trace their roots.'

'Sounds interesting,' said Jamie. 'Can we meet him?'

'Oh, he comes around most days,' said Mrs O'Dea, scraping the remains of the curry into what looked like a dog's dish. What did she have against her dog, I wondered? 'He likes to hang around the stables. Apparently he's a very good rider.'

Oh no, I groaned to myself. Probably doesn't speak much English and is a horse freak. No thanks. My interest cooled quite considerably. All romantic thoughts of playing him off against Jamie went out of the window. Still, I vowed to be nice to the lad. Maybe teach him good English and explain a bit about our Irish culture. He'd be very grateful to me as his mentor and Jamie would get to see me in a glowing new light. I wondered if this David had ever hugged a koala bear. Or maybe eaten one.

2

David

We met David sooner than we expected. At breakfast next morning, Mrs O'Dea glanced through the window.

'There's David now,' she said. 'On his way to the stable yard, no doubt.' She ran to the door and called him. I arranged my face to look kind and benevolent. The effect was somehow lost when David walked in and my jaw dropped open. He was taller than me, for a start. His skin was not the dark colour I'd expected; it was more of a very deep tan, which showed off his magnificent teeth when he grinned at us. His dark hair was close cropped and, the ultimate plus, he sported a silver earring. Now here was someone who knew a thing or two about making an impression. He nodded at each of us as Mrs O'Dea made the introductions. I wished I hadn't dropped my piece of toast on my lap when he focused those eyes on me. I blushed all the way up from my toes as I hastily tried to wipe the marmalade off my jeans. Never mind, I consoled myself. When I got going, teaching David good English and stuff about culture, this moment would be forgotten.

'Been here long, David?' asked Jamie.

'Two weeks,' he replied. 'My mum reached thirty-five this year, so she figured it was time to try and seek her Irish roots. I guess it's her middle-aged gesture towards imm-ortality.'

Once more my jaw hopped off my chest. Not alone was his English perfect, but he had a poetic turn of phrase. It takes one to know one.

'Why don't you kids go on out?' said Mrs O'Dea. 'After

washing-up,' she added.

My impression of Mrs O'Dea as a comfy lady with comfy culinary skills and a comfy motherliness was fast fading. Still, the washing-up gave me a chance to surreptitiously wipe the marmalade off my jeans.

We made our way down the road, a bit self-conscious because of the newcomer to our group. I knocked the suggestion that we go up to the stables.

'Let's see a bit of the landscape,' I said, with a graceful gesture towards the flat fields. Anything was better than horses. Nobody objected, which established me in a sort of leader role. As it should.

'There's a nice river through those trees,' said David. 'We could go there.'

So we climbed over a gate and followed David down to a river bank. We skimmed stones and then raced leaves – letting them off together and chasing after them. Before we realised it, we'd gone miles downstream. Exhausted, we collapsed on the bank.

'I wonder what's over there,' said Leo, pointing to the bank on the far side which was hidden by thick foliage. 'Looks interesting.'

'Probably much the same as what's here only it's covered with those bushes,' I said.

'We could get across,' said Jamie. 'Look, the river narrows just at that bend. We could easily cross.'

'Don't be so childish,' I said. 'Let's go back and listen to some of my CDs – I've brought the best with me.'

David looked undecided. I knew I could swing him with a bit of eyelash flapping, but that made me lose my balance and I slid down to the water's edge. The other three didn't need any prompting. They were beside me in a flash; not to save me should I fall in and drown tragically, but to feel

their way along the uneven stones that lay across this part
of the river. I had no choice but to follow. At one stage
David reached out and took my hand. That made my
spirits soar. Perhaps crossing the river was a good idea
after all if it made for physical contact. I turned to make
sure that Jamie saw this macho gesture. Big mistake.
Didn't see the gap between the stones and put my foot
right into the water.

'Me good runners!' I exclaimed. I'd saved for weeks for
these. 'Bloody hell!'

Poets shouldn't swear. 'I don't normally swear,' I muttered.

Leo laughed. 'Not half. You should hear her when she's
really upset, David. She'd light up a town.'

Me and my big mouth. Maybe that was my tragic thing.
Where the other women poets had to contend with
tuberculosis and all that stuff, maybe my burden was my
motor-mouth. When they'd write my epitaph they'd say,
'She was a wonderful poet, tragically afflicted by a mouth
which betrayed her beautiful mind.' Or words to that
effect. Right now I had to concentrate on getting across
the rest of the way without making an eejit of myself.

Jamie reached out and pulled me over the last stretch.
That was two lots of boys' hands I'd held today and it was
still only eleven o'clock.

'Deadly,' said Leo, making his way through the foliage.
'It's like the jungle. Come on.'

We followed him, keeping his skinny form in sight as he
forged ahead. After a while we came to a clearing in front of
a hill. Again Leo was ahead of us. After first checking that
there were no hairy beasts in our line of vision, I followed
the boys. When I caught up with them, they were standing
at the top of the hill, looking at something below.

'Wow!' I said, following their gaze. 'What a smashing place.'

And so it was. Nestling down in the valley stood an old Georgian house. Even at this distance we could see that it was very neglected, but it must have been lovely once. We could see the remains of a tennis court that was now over-run with weeds. In front of the house was a sweeping avenue which disappeared behind a clump of rhododendron bushes. There were nine windows upstairs and three on either side of the imposing front door below. A big arch led into a yard where there were, yes of course, the inevitable stables. Except that, thankfully, there was no sign of a horse. The stables looked like they hadn't been used in years, some of the doors were hanging off. All around the estate there were oak trees and big chestnut trees that spread out with great majesty.

'I wonder if anyone lives there,' said Jamie. 'What say we have a look?'

'Fine by me,' I said. Leo was nodding too. We looked at David and were surprised to see him sitting on the grass, elbows on knees and his chin cupped in his hands. He was looking very intently at the house, a sort of lost look on his face. I supposed it was because they wouldn't have much in the line of Georgian houses in Australia, it being pretty new and all that.

'David?' prompted Jamie. 'You interested?'

'What? Oh!' With that David snapped from his daydream and jumped up. 'Sure thing,' he said.

We ran down the hill towards the house, amazed at how big it seemed the nearer we got to it. We'd almost reached the sweep of the front avenue when a shot rang out.

Crows on the nearby chestnut trees squawked as they flapped in a scattering of raggedy black over our heads.

At first we weren't quite sure that it *was* a gunshot. It could have been a car backfiring. But when a man with a shotgun appeared at the arch that led to the stables we knew that trouble was in the offing. A skinny old geezer he was, with heavy grey eyebrows that almost covered his eyes, and wild grey hair that stuck out from around his bald crown.

'What are you lot doing here?' he roared. 'This is private property. Get off my land.' With those words of welcome he fired another shot into the air. I read in a magazine once that adrenaline is stuff inside you that's released in times of danger or stress. It comes from prehistoric times when man had to face big scaly creatures and this adrenaline made him fight or flee. No argument here; flight was the rule of the moment. Even the squelching of my soaking runner didn't stop me from passing out the others. My adrenaline was on overdrive. Another shot rang out and, I'm ashamed to admit, I didn't check to see if any of the boys had been hit.

Gasping for breath, we didn't stop until we were over the hill and out of range. We threw ourselves down in a wheezing heap. Leo peered over the top, like one of those soldiers in the trenches in World War One.

'He hasn't followed us,' he said. 'We're safe now.'

'Stupid maniac!' exclaimed Jamie. 'Who the hell is he?'

David shrugged. 'Beats me,' he said. 'I've only been here a couple of weeks. I didn't even know that old house was there. You can't see it from the road.'

'It looks like a haunted old dump to me,' I said, taking off my runner to wring out my wet sock. 'Probably is, haunted I mean. That old ghoul is probably a descendant of Dracula. He has vampire written all over him. Doesn't he know he shouldn't leave his box during daylight?'

'More of a geriatric cowboy, if you ask me,' said David. 'Thinks we're trying to stake a claim on his territory.'

'Come on,' said Jamie, getting up and wiping grass stains from his jeans. 'No point in hanging about here waiting for him to head us off at the pass and take a shot at us. Let's get back.'

With the odd backward glance, just to be sure that the old geezer hadn't crept up on us, we made our way back across the river. Hands reached out to help me again. Only this time it was Leo, which was a waste, so I got across under my own steam.

'Let's go back to the cottage,' said David, with his attractive Australian drawl. 'We can have a coke and chill out.'

That was talking my language. 'Great,' I said. I stuck out my chin and looked at the other two, daring them to suggest something active, like exploring or, heaven forbid, interacting with creatures of the equine breed. But they seemed happy with David's invitation.

The cottage that David and his mother were renting was about a quarter of a mile beyond the lodge. It wasn't really a cottage – more an old house that had been added to over the years. There was a big garden, where you wouldn't take your dog in case he dug up a dahlia or left something nasty and steaming on the grass.

'Nice place,' I said, with all the flattery due to someone who's going to give you coke and a place to chill out. 'Must be costing a bomb to rent.'

David shook his head. 'It's not costing us anything,' he said. 'It's a swap.'

'A swap?' I asked.

'Yes,' he went on. 'Mum is a member of an international house-swapping association. You pay a fee to have your house in a catalogue, offering it as an exchange. Mum has been wanting to come to Ireland for ages, so she – we – were thrilled when the owner here agreed to a swap.'

'Cool,' I said. Now why couldn't my folks do something like that instead of the usual dreary old caravan in Tramore. Where it nearly always rained.

'Mum's gone to town,' said David. 'Make yourselves at home.'

That was no bother to us. We sprawled on the comfy sofas. Pity they were covered with white fabric as my damp trainer left a muddy mark. Leo noticed and sniggered. I tried to wipe it off before David came back from the kitchen, but it just spread, so I sat on it.

'What's all this stuff?' asked Jamie, looking through papers which were scattered on the table.

'Oh, they're Mum's notes,' replied David, coming from the kitchen with coke and crisps. 'Like I told you, she's heavy into family roots and all that stuff. Personally I think it's a waste of time. But it keeps her happy and I got to come here. Got to meet you folks.'

I hoped he didn't notice the deep blush that crept all over my face. I was sure he meant me. Just me.

THE DARK ROMEO

By Maeve Morris

He looked at me, my Ozzie love.
Made my heart flutter like a dove.
He came so far to seek my hand.
My head resounds like a brass band.

'Mrs O'Dea says you're part Aborigine,' said Leo. 'Is that right?'

I was mortified. Now David knew we'd been talking about him before we'd even met him. But he just laughed.

'That's right,' he replied. 'Mum thinks my grandfather came from around these parts.'

'Don't you know?' I asked. 'Most people at least know where their grandparents came from, whatever about relations farther back. I can trace my ancestors back to Brian Boru. On my father's side,' I added, as Leo snorted. 'Nothing to do with your side.'

'No,' David replied to my question. 'Grandpa wouldn't ever talk about his past. If I asked him, he'd change the subject. Mum just has a few hazy facts to go on about the Irish connection. I don't know why she's bothered.'

'But how come ...?' began Jamie. He blushed scarlet and fiddled with his coke can. 'I mean ...' he fumbled for words again. This was fun. It was nice to see articulate, cultured Jamie, who had the answer to everything, shuffle with embarrassment. Made him more human. I was enjoying this.

'You mean where does the Aboriginal bit come in?' laughed David.

Jamie looked relieved. He had that British inhibition about race and colour and trying not to offend. As if any of that stuff mattered. I wished someone in my family had had a bit of dark colour, then I wouldn't be plagued with cruddy freckles and skin the colour of a dead mackerel's belly.

Jamie nodded. 'Just wondered,' he muttered.

David laughed again. 'All I know about Grandpa Kelly is that he went out to Australia in the nineteen-twenties and built Greatwell Station.'

'A station?' asked Leo. 'Was he a navvie?'

David looked at him with a puzzled expression. Then he grinned.

'Not a railway station, you wally,' he laughed. 'A sheep station – sheep farm. He worked hard at it. Didn't bother much with the social niceties – you know the sort of thing.'

'No,' I said, intrigued by words like 'sheep station' and 'social niceties'.

'Oh,' said David impatiently. 'A couple of times a year there would be a big social gathering on one sheep station or another. Families came from hundreds of miles for a few days dancing and all that stuff. It was really just a way of offloading daughters on suitable matches. Ghastly, it must have been.'

'That's very sexist,' I remarked. 'There's no way I'd have let my parents offload me on to some whiskery old fogey with a few maggotty sheep and a homestead.'

'A few sheep?' echoed Leo. 'Maeve, you're talking thousands and thousands of sheep and thousands and thousands of acres. Anyway,' he added, with a silly grin, 'even if you'd been around then, nobody would have taken you on. You'd have driven any bloke mental.'

'Go on, David,' I said with cool dignity.

'Well, my grandfather had no time for all that,' he went on. 'He was middle-aged when he met my grandmother. She was the daughter of his stockman.'

'An Aborigine, this stockman?' I asked.

David nodded. 'Ben Yagam. He'd been with Grandpa from the beginning. He taught him everything there was to know about the land. Taught him how to live *with* the land, not against it. Best tracker in the whole region ...'

'His daughter,' I put in. 'Get back to the stockman's daughter and your grandfather.'

'Nothing much,' said David, taking a gulp from his coke can. 'They met, fell in luuuvvve, ha ha, and got married. And my mum was born. Just Mum. No more children. Grandma died when Mum was little.'

'Oh no,' I gasped. 'There must be more to the story than that. What was her name? What did she look like? Why did she die? Was your grandfather heartbroken?'

'Easy on,' laughed David. 'Her name was Boalere. She fell off a horse – which was a freak accident because she was a brilliant rider – got a fever and never recovered. End of story.'

'Oh, that's so sad,' I said. 'Stupid horses.'

'How come you're called Kelly?' asked Leo. 'It's your mother who's a Kelly and women change their name when they marry. Right? How come you don't have your dad's name?'

Trust Leo's brain to have been clicking over the practalities while I concentrated on the romantic.

David crushed his empty can and tossed it into the sink

with a clatter. He turned to look at Leo in a sort of challenging way.

"But my mum never married,' he said.

'Oh, I see,' said Leo. Now it was his turn to be embarrassed. Thank goodness it was he who'd asked the question and not me.

David let the embarrassed pause ride for a few moments before he laughed.

'I'm the result of a student affair,' he said. 'Mum met my father while she was at university. She studied Anglo-Irish literature,' he added proudly. 'Just to please Grandpa really. He was always talking about Ireland, even though he'd never talk about his family. She met my father while she was in third year. The affair didn't last, but I was the by-product. Mum refused to marry him. Said they'd be getting married for the wrong reasons and that they'd both end up miserable. Besides, she had all the support she wanted from Grandpa Kelly and Ben.'

'And what became of him?' asked Leo. 'Your father?'

'The Great White Shark,' laughed David. 'He's okay. He's a geneticist in Melbourne. Which makes for interesting conversation when he introduces me as his son.'

'Why is that?' asked Leo.

'Well, him being someone who is involved in researching origins of races and species, it takes a bit of explaining how he comes to have a mixed-race son.'

'Is that a problem?' I asked.

David laughed again. 'No,' he said. 'I get along fine with his wife and my two half-sisters. I live with them for part of the year, the rest of the time I spend with Mum.'

I sighed. Imagine having a father who is married to someone other than your mum. Weird. I thought about my own old man and wondered if I'd trade him for a more upmarket brand of father. But then I decided not. He drives my mother and me around the twist, but, when you overlook his daft humour and seventies time-warp, he's okay – so long as I don't expose my friends to him for longer than is necessary.

'And your mother never fell in love again?' I asked.

David snorted. 'Love? Yecchh. Yeah, sure. She's had men take her to fancy dinners and the theatre, but no one special. She's happy with her life.'

I sighed again. There was more romance in this boy's life than I could ever write in a lifetime of romantic poetry.

'So that's why I'm still a Kelly,' continued David. 'Maybe that's why Mum is so anxious that I get to know all about my ancestors. She feels she owes it to me to make up for not having a real family, as she calls it. But it doesn't matter to me. Though I always felt very close to Grandpa Kelly. I don't really remember Ben, my Aboriginal great-grandad. He died when I was just little.'

'Did you live on the sheep farm with your grandad?' I asked. 'When it was your turn to live with your mum, I mean.'

'Only for the past five years,' David replied. 'Mum had a job teaching in Melbourne University and we had a smashing apartment. But then Grandpa Kelly got ill. After Ben had died, he wore himself out trying to keep things going. Eventually he collapsed and became an invalid.'

'What became of the sheep station?' asked practical Leo.

'Mum gave up her job at the university and came back to nurse him and to try and manage the business, but ...' he shrugged. 'It started to go downhill, what with bushfires and the price of sheep and all that. There was no way that Mum could manage Greatwell Station. But then she got this crazy notion that she could make it a sort of bush tourist place. Her heart was always set on running a hotel or guest house. She poured most of her inheritance money into converting the workmen's huts into self-catering units and advertised in the papers. She thought people like writers and artists would come. You know the type, bonding with nature and all that garbage.'

'Totally brilliant,' I said. 'I'd love to stay in a place like that. Did they come, the artists and writers?'

'Nah,' said David. 'Only a few straggling oddbods who wanted a swimming-pool and entertainment. Out in the bush? Airheads! The whole deal was a write-off.'

'Oh no,' I said. 'After all her trouble. What did she do?'

'Sold out,' replied David. 'At a loss too. We moved back to Melbourne, but we couldn't afford the same sort of apartment as we had before. We're renting a small house in the suburbs. Anyway, here we are,' he gestured around the room. 'Mum has always been conscious of her Irishness. Says it's her Celtic blood that makes her creative, and her Aboriginal roots that connect her with nature.'

'What happened your grandad?' asked Jamie.

'He died three years ago,' said David. 'Just as well really. He'd have been heartbroken to see his farm dwindle away and sold off. Look, could we steer this away from me. I'm bored talking about me. What about you lot?'

Jamie, Leo and I shuffled a bit. How could we match David's story? Well, I could have spiced up my own ancestral past into a sort of *Pride and Prejudice* meets *Sleepless in Seattle*. But Leo would have blown my story away.

'Nothing to tell, really,' said Jamie eventually. 'We're pretty ordinary folk by your standards.'

'And that's the truth,' I added.

3

Roots

That night we watched a video in Mrs O'Dea's. She went out to bingo and left us a plate of ham sandwiches, which I fell on like a famine victim because the Hungarian goulash we'd had for dinner was more like gristle soaked in muck. But the ham sandwiches were bad news for Leo because he's a vegetarian. He gave me his ham and just ate the bread and the salad bits, so for once I didn't call him a veggie freak.

We didn't ask David any more about his past because Jamie said he might think we were too nosy. So when the video was over we just played loud music until Mrs O'Dea came back. Then we walked David to his place and sang a rude Australian ballad he'd taught us.

That night I thought about David and all that he'd told us. It was time to add to the Poetry Book, which I kept hidden inside the covers of an old *Woman's Way* just in case Leo came nosing about. I imagined discovering that my real father was some exotic figure far away.

THE GYPSY FATHER

By Maeve Morris

I never knew my wandering Da.
He roamed away to lands quite far.
He played the sax and courted girls,
With his yummy eyes and golden curls.
I wish he'd come and play for me,
And take me off across the sea.

I wish he'd tell me," Daughter dear,
Hang in there, kid, I'll soon be near.
We'll roam the world, see all we can,
In our new and fancy caravan.'

Next morning we called to David's place after breakfast. That was my idea; I wanted to see how this mother with the romantic past measured up. As it happened she was everything I'd imagined. Her skin was a shade darker than David's. Her hair was cut close to her head, her elegant neck – not unlike my own – was emphasised by the silver earrings that swayed as she moved. She was wearing a loose white tunic with a wide leather belt over white trousers. Thong sandals showed off blue-varnished toe-nails. And when she smiled at us with warm friendliness, I knew she'd passed the Maeve Morris Acceptable Adult Test.

'You must be Mrs O'Dea's guests,' she said.

Mrs O'Dea's guests. I liked that. This lady was doing just fine.

'Hi, Mrs ... er ...Kelly,' said Leo, getting all tangled up over her name. David's mum laughed with the same hearty laugh as her son.

'Call me Eppie,' she said.

'Eppie? Is that short for something?' I asked.

She nodded. 'Short for Epona.'

'Epona. An Aboriginal name?'

She shook her head. 'You don't know your Celtic mythology, dear,' she said.

'Epona is Celtic?' I wished now I'd read the bits of Celtic folklore that had been printed on the backs of our milk cartons over several weeks.

'Epona was a Celtic horse goddess,' put in David.

'Oh, that Epona,' I said, trying to look knowledgeable, but only digging a deeper pit of embarrassment.

Eppie laughed. 'Oh, my father – he loved to read Celtic stories and he loved horses. He stuck that name on me.'

'Isn't that ironic?' said Leo.

'Excuse me?' said Eppie. I was still trying to work out what ironic meant.

'Isn't it ironic that you were called after a horse goddess and then your mother dies from a fall off a horse?'

Eppie looked surprised and glanced at her son, as if wondering how this bunch of strangers knew so much about her background. But it didn't bother her.

'True,' she said. 'Bit of a twist of fate there all right.' Then she began rustling her notes, putting them in order.

'Have you got very far?' asked Jamie, nodding towards the notes.

Eppie sighed as she tapped them on the table to even out the bundle of pages.

'Not very far, I'm afraid. I wish I'd asked my father much more before he passed away.'

'But you did, Mum,' put in David. 'You tried to, many times, but he'd always clam up whenever we'd ask about his ancestors. *Our* ancestors,' he added bitterly. 'It was as if he wanted to forget about his own people, even though he loved everything Irish. You're wasting your time.'

Eppie frowned. 'So you keep telling me, David,' she said, a tad sharply. 'But I want to do this. I know my Aboriginal background inside out, but I need to know my connections with this side of the world. To complete the circle, as it were, and tell me who I really am. And you too, David. It's important for you too.'

David snorted. 'I know who I am,' he said. 'I'm just happy being me. I don't care about all that ancestral stuff.

It's a big bore, Mum. Leave it. Get out and get a life.'

His mother shook her head. 'There we differ,' she said.

I could see that all this was a sore point between mother and son. In a way I sided with David; it seemed like an awful lot of trouble just to figure out a bunch of dead people. But I could also see Eppie's point. Coming as she did from two very different ethnic groups, I figured she was looking for some sort of an identity for herself and her son. Heavy stuff, all right.

'Anyway,' went on Eppie, standing up, 'I'm going into Newbridge. If you folks want lunch, there are fish fingers and oven chips in the freezer?'

While David began cooking, Jamie looked curiously at the bundle of notes Eppie had left on the table.

'Wow!' he said. 'Your mum certainly knows how to research, David.'

David looked up from the heap of chips he was piling on to an oven tray. 'She's used to that kind of thing.'

'Who's Dan Donnelly?' went on Jamie, pointing to a page he'd pulled from the bundle.

David gave another scornful snort. 'He's nobody,' he said. 'Before he died my grandfather went ga-ga. For no reason he'd start boxing the air with his fists, shouting "Dan Donnelly! Dan Donnelly!" Then he'd lean towards me, grab my arm and say, "Dan Donnelly – the Kelly pride and joy." It was just mad old folk talk, but Mum has latched on to that name. Like I said, total waste of time. Who wants fish fingers?'

'Can you fry an egg for Leo?' I asked. Well, I was feeling in a generous mood.

Jamie's grandad was waiting for us when we got back to the lodge that evening. He was uneasily trying to balance a cup of tea and a slice of Mrs O'Dea's perfectly gruesome sunken fruitcake on his lap. When he smiled with delight at our noisy arrival, I could see bits of sticky raisin stuck to his teeth.

'Well, you lot,' he said jovially. 'Having a good time?'

'Great,' we said in unison. Which was true. In fact I'd quite forgotten about him and the house up the avenue.

'The Montgomerys have invited you up for dinner this evening,' went on Mr McLaren, looking at Jamie. 'Eight o'clock all right?'

'Good,' I whispered, winking at Jamie and nodding towards the kitchen where Mrs O'Dea was clattering about. 'Bring us back something nice in a doggy bag.'

'But you're all invited,' said Mr McLaren. 'All three.'

That caused me to gasp in mid-breath. Now here was a whole set of problems laid on me. What would I wear? Who would be there? Would I get get nervous, at a table set with too many spoons and forks? Would I be put sitting with some whiskery bore who'd want to talk about horses' fetlocks and forelocks? No, thank you very much. I'd have much preferred to run the risk of Mrs O'Dea's cooking than to go on display at a poncy dinner-party.

'Oh no, Mr McLaren,' I said in my ever-so-polite voice for special wheedling. 'They're your friends, yours and Jamie's. Leo and I will be quite happy to stay here. Really.'

I knew Leo was eyeing me with dismay, but I ignored him. I knew he'd be dead chuffed to trundle off to this dinner with his scrubbed face and beguiling conversation and have everyone say what a delightful and intelligent boy he was, coochee coo. Mr McLaren laughed and put down the tea and unfinished cake. 'Don't be silly, Maeve,' he said. 'They're dying to meet you all. See you at eight then.'

He shouted a bright 'Cheerio' to Mrs O'Dea and let

himself out at the front door. We looked at one another.

'Great,' grinned Jamie. 'The food up there is really smashing.'

'Totally excellent,' laughed Leo.

'Yeah,' I said.

'That's a very flat "yeah", Maeve,' said Jamie. 'Don't you want to come?'

I bit my lip. I didn't want to appear ungrateful or rude. 'I just don't know what to wear,' I said.

'Just wear what you normally wear,' said Jamie. 'It's no big deal, Maeve.'

Oh yes, it was. As we watched MTV for a bit, how I longed to stay put, curled up on the sofa with crisps and chocolate and forget about the cruddy dinner. But Mrs O'Dea was making quite sure that we'd be on time.

'Up you get,' she said, pressing the remote and turning off Robbie Williams in mid-throttle.

I put everything I'd brought out on the bed. Jeans would be out, for a start. That left combats and a pair of black trousers that Mum had insisted I pack. I went for the black. Then I rifled through my tops. They were mostly tee-shirts with pictures of characters from *South Park*, *The Simpsons*, and stuff like that. I finally settled on the *South Park* one. If I wore my blue shirt over it, nobody would guess my wardrobe consisted mainly of American TV shows. I spat on my Docs and polished them with loo paper. Then I caught my hair up in a clutch comb to show off my elegant neck. There, I'd do. Ready for battle, I came down to where Jamie was teaching Leo to play poker. Leo looked up.

'About time,' he said. 'We've been ready for ages.'

Jamie stood up. 'Wow!' he said. 'You look really smashing, Maeve. Really cool.'

'Huh, this old thing?' I said. But I was dead pleased. Let the Montgomerys do their worst, but Jamie thought I looked cool. Some things are more important than others.

We ambled up the avenue. It was still warm and bright. I took off my shirt so that it wouldn't get creased before we'd reach the house. Across a field some birds were warbling a sort of jingly sound. I kind of wished Leo could be beamed away from here and that it was just Jamie and me. The whole scene smacked of romantic sophistication – warbling birds, big avenue, me and Jamie looking beautiful, going to a grown-up dinner party, even if it was a poncy one. It was one of those moments that you want to freeze so that you can pull it out again and again to savour its lyrical feeling.

'I can see the shape of your knickers through those pants,' said Leo.

All my beautiful thoughts just withered and died. I spluttered with rage.

'You're dead,' I said, gritting my teeth. 'As soon as this is over, you're dead.'

'But it's true,' he persisted. 'Look, I can see the ridges. Can't you see them, Jamie?'

Now I was completely livid. How dare he draw attention to the shape of my knickers. How dare he even mention the word in front of Jamie. To make it worse, Jamie was *looking*! He was shaking his head.

'Can't see anything,' he said.

I struggled into my shirt, still foaming at the mouth and snarling at Leo. The madder I got the more he enjoyed it.

'You've ruined everything,' I almost sobbed. 'I'll never relax now. I think I'll just go back and brave Mrs O'Dea's slop. Go on, you two. Besides, I wouldn't be seen dead with you, Leo louse.'

Jamie caught my arm. 'I've told you, Maeve,' he said. 'You look just great. Don't mind Leo.'

He was right. I scowled very meaningfully at smirking Leo and faced back up the avenue. We walked in silence for a while.

'Here we are,' said Jamie. Rounding a bend we came on the big ivy-covered house that was Briarstown Stud. If I had an architect's manual I could describe the windows and porch pillars properly, point out the fancy things along the roof and mention the curvy brick bits on either side. Suffice to say that it was big and it was old. But my heart sank when I saw the number of cars parked outside. I hoped that all these people wouldn't want to talk to me and that none of them would see the shape of my underwear if I kept my shirt pulled down.

4
High Life

The loud chattering was the first thing that hit us when we shuffled into the big hall. A gushing lady descended on Jamie and smothered him with in an embrace. He looked helplessly at me over her shoulder and I made a kissy-kissy face at him.

'Mrs Montgomery,' he said, when she released him, 'this is Maeve and Leo.'

'Charming, charming,' she laughed. 'And how are you enjoying life at the dower house?'

Even Leo was stumped at this one.

'It's not dour at all,' I said. 'It's lovely. Lots of mad colours. It's really bright. I love it. I don't know why you'd think it's dour.'

'Of course, dear,' smiled Mrs M. 'Jamie dear, you know some of the guests, introduce your friends.' Then she tootled off, leaving us to the mercy of the chattering masses.

'What's a dower house?' Leo asked.

'It's the nickname for the lodge,' Jamie explained. 'A dower house is usually a house on a large estate where a widowed aristocrat goes to live when she hands over the house to the heir.'

'It doesn't mean drab?' I gasped. 'Are you saying that dower doesn't mean drab?'

Jamie grinned as he shook his head. 'I think you're confusing it with the word dour,' he said, pronouncing it 'dooer'. 'Different thing altogether.'

'Oh God,' I groaned. 'Great start.'

'Don't worry, Maeve,' said Jamie. 'Mrs Montgomery is

hyper. She tosses out lots of "charmings" and "luvvies" but doesn't notice what people are saying.'

'That's not much comfort,' I muttered. 'She must think I'm a right eejit.'

Apart from a few freaky odd-bods who neighed loudly across their wine glasses, the rest of the guests were okay. After the usual mindless questions about school, native county and what sort of music we were into, they pretty much left us alone. Especially when I joked about the dower house, now that I knew what it was.

'We're staying with Lady Dower,' I joked. Which was pretty humorous, I thought.

At dinner we were put sitting together. That was a relief – except that Leo was between Jamie and me. The food was magic. The smoked salmon starters would have done me just fine as a dinner, but when chicken in some sort of sauce with grassy bits in it was wheeled in I was in heaven.

'Wine, madam?' I looked up to see a Luke Goss look-alike wielding a wine bottle in my direction.

'Me?' I said. I looked at Jamie, who was nodding and smiling. Hell, I thought. Why not? 'Thank you,' I said, bold as you like, as if I did this sort of thing every day. This was just so sophisticated. I watched as the red liquid was poured into my glass, feeling that there should be cameras and an orchestra. Leo turned up his nose and asked for a coke, but Jamie took the wine. We looked at one another and grinned. This was a very grown-up moment. Meaningful, romantic and significant.

'Barry,' a voice rang out. It was Mrs Montgomery, sitting at the top of the table. 'The children will have soft drinks, Barry.'

All heads turned to look at us. Die? I wished a hole would appear and swallow me. Leo looked smug and

innocent with his coke in front of him as the wine was whipped away from Jamie and me. I blushed all the way to my toes, as if I'd been caught in a shop with my hands in the till.

'You nearly got away with that,' said the geezer on the other side of me. He had a youngish face marred only by a bushy moustache which made him look like a cross between a Spanish dancer and a Mafia hitman.

'I wasn't trying to get away with anything,' I retorted. 'It's not my fault if that daft waiter thinks I'm older than I am.'

He laughed and raised his glass to me. 'You're a spirited little lady,' he said. 'Here,' he held out his glass towards me. 'You can have a sip of mine if you like.'

I looked at his moustache and declined graciously. I wouldn't want to sip anything that this stranger's hairy upper lip had been trawling – I had my health to think of.

However, the gesture broke the ice and soon we were talking like old friends. He told me his name was Frank Jellet and he was an estate agent.

'You own one of those shops with little pictures of houses in the window?' I said, just so that he'd know I knew what an estate agent was.

'Something like that,' he laughed.

'Cool,' I said. 'You get to see the insides of all those houses, then?'

'Upstairs, downstairs and in my lady's chamber.'

'Huh?'

'Like in the nursery rhyme,' he went on. 'Goosey goosey gander?''

'Never heard of him,' I said, wondering what a goose would be doing in a lady's chamber. Funny the things people come out with sometimes. Perhaps it was as well I hadn't had any of that wine.

'That's my uncle over there,' Frank said, nodding towards a blocky middle-aged man across the table. 'Uncle Edgar.'

Uncle Edgar caught us looking at him and he waved cheerily. His forehead ran all the way over his head, unfettered by a single strand of hair. His plump body wobbled when he laughed, and he was doing a lot of that. Laughing, I mean. I could get to like this nephew and his cheerful uncle, I thought.

Frank went on to tell me that he'd spent three years after he qualified back-packing and working around the world.

'That's just what I'd love to do,' I said. 'When I qualify,' I added, just to give my intentions a bit of class.

'Qualify as what?' asked Frank, knocking the wind out of my sails. Qualify as what indeed? 'I mean, what do you want to do when you leave school?' he went on.

I nearly said that my sole ambition at the moment was just to do that – leave school, but that would not have been a sophisticated reply.

'I thought about studying Anglo-Irish literature,' I said grandly, as if I actually knew what Anglo-Irish literature was. But Eppie had done it, so it must be good.

'Oh, a literary lady,' said Frank. 'I'm impressed.'

Well, before I knew it I was telling him about my poetry and how hard it is sometimes to get things to rhyme. I told him about Emily Dickinson using slashes instead of full stops because it always amazes people that I know that.

'Of course I always use full stops and things myself,' I added. 'My poems make sense.'

'My goodness, Maeve Morris,' he said. 'I'll be watching out for your name on tomes and anthologies in the future. Another Eavan Boland in the making.'

'I suppose,' I smiled, making a mental note to look up the words 'tomes' and 'anthologies' to see if they were good things. And who was Eavan Boland? 'Tell me, Frank,' I went on, changing the subject in case he pulled out any more words and names that would leave me looking blank, 'when you were back-packing, did you ever get to Australia by any chance?'

'I certainly did,' he replied. 'I spent four glorious months there. Smashing country. I'd recommend it. You'd write lots of poems there, Maeve.'

By now the rest of my chicken had gone cold, but it didn't matter because here I was – at a grown-up dinner party – talking to a man who had travelled the world. As the dessert trolley came round, I was beginning to wonder if he'd fallen for my elegant neck and high-class conversation, or was he humouring me as a kid he was stuck with. It's a difficult age, this. But the profiteroles drizzled with delightfully sticky cobwebs of toffee banished that thought.

'Isn't it a coincidence that I'm sitting here talking to someone who has been to Australia,' I said. 'Because I have just met an Australian boy who's here with his mother. They're trying to trace their Irish ancestry.'

'Really?' said Frank. 'What's the name?'

'Kelly,' I replied, licking a splodge of cream off my lip. 'All they know is that David's grandfather emigrated in 1925. They think he was born around here. They don't know any more than that because Eppie – that's the mother – Eppie's father never spoke about his Irish ancestry. Which is strange, because he loved everything Irish.' I was about to add that that was why Eppie studied Anglo-Irish literature, but that would have diminished my ambitious boast. 'David, that's the son, doesn't really care about the past. It's his mother who has this mad need to find their roots.'

Frank nodded. 'That could be a difficult task,' he said. 'Especially if they haven't much to go on. There must be hundreds of Kellys from this area alone who emigrated.'

'It's a very romantic story,' I went on. 'David's grand-father fell in love with an Aborigine lady and he married her but she fell off a horse and was killed, leaving her small daughter, David's mother. He never married again because he loved her so much. Isn't that just so sad?'

Just as the coffee was being served, and just as I was glancing at Jamie to see if he was noticing me engrossed in conversation with an older male, there was a slight disturbance.

'Jack!' exclaimed Mrs Montgomery, wiping her mouth delicately on her napkin and getting up from the table.

Everyone looked to see who had just come in.

At first I couldn't see because Mrs Montgomery was leaning forward, patting the newcomer on the shoulder. But when she stood back, I nearly choked on my hot coffee when I saw who it was. Leo nudged me in the ribs.

'Look,' he whispered. 'It's him.'

The late arrival was the garrulous old trigger-happy freak who'd run us off his land.

Jamie reached over and tapped my free hand, my other hand was holding my napkin to my face.

'Don't worry, Maeve,' he whispered. 'I don't think he'll recognise us. Just stay cool.'

'Jack, Jack,' Mrs Montgomery laughed as she led the man to the place which had been set for him. 'You do this to me every time. Come along, I'll get them to feed you.'

Thankfully he was sitting at the far end, away from us. After a few nods and waves, everyone resumed chatting.

'Who is that old codg ... old man?' I asked Frank.

Frank laughed. 'That's old Jack,' he said. ' Jack Horton, an eccentric recluse. The wonder is that he came here at all. He normally shuns this sort of thing. Phyllis – Mrs Montgomery – always asks him for old time's sake. Her father-in-law used to play chess with the old man. He's a harmless old hermit, but you wouldn't want to cross his path unless you've a very good reason. He can be quite paranoid about his property.'

'Paranoid!' I blurted out before I could control my mouth. 'He's a dangerous ...'

Leo, who had been listening, dug me in the ribs again. 'Sshh,' he hissed. I checked myself and cleared my throat. Luckily Frank's attention was focused on holding out his cup for coffee. Leo was right; there was no need to draw attention to the fact that we'd been chased from Jack's land, in case people would think we'd been harassing the old guy.

The three of us kept ourselves out of Dangerous Jack's focus for the rest of the evening. In fact we left when the dinner-party broke up and people were circulating with fiddly little glasses of liqueurs – which we weren't offered.

'So now we at least know his name,' said Jamie as we headed for the lodge. 'And that he's crazy. The message is to keep clear of him.'

'That's what Frank said,' I put in.

'Frank?' Jamie looked at me quizzically.

'My friend, Frank,' I went on. 'He's an estate agent and can talk poetry. Very nice fellow. Very cultured.'

Jamie smiled indulgently, but I felt sure he was mad jealous inside his head. At least I hoped he was. According to Mills and Boon, he should be.

THE MACHO LOVER

By Maeve Morris

Jack the Bandit came to town,
Made the gentle maiden frown
As with his gun he ran amok
Shooting bullets, pok, pok, pok.
'Don't worry, lass,' said Sheriff Frank.
'I'll deal with him, the evil crank.
I'll hang him from the highest tree
So from his pestering you'll be free.'
'Oh, Frank my love,' the maiden sighed.
'You are so strong, with you I'll bide.
Despite your very hairy lips,
I'll bake you buns and pies and chips.'

5

Donnelly's Hollow

Next morning, when David called round, he had riding-boots on. I groaned within. No doubt the other two would want to ride their hobby horses too. Of course I was right.

'Sure, we'd love to ride out,' said Jamie. Leo nodded eagerly.

'Not me,' I said, getting my spoke in early.

Leo scowled at me. 'Here we go again,' he said. 'Mighty Maeve wanting us to coax her so that she'll feel important.'

'No,' I said. 'I really mean it. I can't stand horses. They're big, they're mean and they roll their eyes at you.' *And they've been known to kill people's mothers*, I could have added. But I didn't say it. I do have some decorum.

'You three go ahead,' I went on, in a very reasonable tone of voice so that I couldn't be accused of throwing a tantrum. 'I know you want to. I really don't mind.'

There was an awkward pause. Then Mrs O'Dea got up and started gathering the breakfast things.

'Why don't you come into Newbridge with me, Maeve,' she said. 'I'm going shopping. We could have coffee and buns when we're finished.'

Shopping! Now that sounded a bit more like my sort of thing. That and buns. And so it was settled. The boys ran up the avenue, leaping about like little kids. They could have shown a bit more regret at my not accompanying them, I thought. One likes to be missed.

With gears screaming, Mrs O'Dea eased the car on to the road, narrowly avoiding a tractor. I thought if her driving was anything like her cooking, I might have been safer on the back of some nag. But we made it to town, and shopped in a big shopping centre. When Mrs O'Dea told me that the Montgomerys were paying for our food, I made sure to suggest things like oven chips and ready-made meals – things that even she couldn't damage much. I also got some blue nail varnish and hair glitter – in case there might be more of those dinners.

Afterwards we walked through the town. Mrs O'Dea was wearing her usual cords, a green windcheater with matching wellies, a flame-red cotton jumper and a striped woollen hat. I hoped nobody would think she was my granny. Or, worse still, my mother.

'You like bright colours, Mrs O'Dea,' I said. 'Don't you?'

'I do, lass,' she replied. 'Since I was sixteen years old I worked at Briarstown, when old Mr and Mrs Montgomery ruled the roost. In those days everyone knew their place. Respect, dear, that was it. You don't get that sort of respect nowadays.'

'What has that to do with liking bright colours?' I asked.

'Well,' she said, 'up to the time I retired I always wore black. Black dress, black overalls, black stockings. It was the normal thing for people in service then, black was. When I was widowed twenty-five years ago, I didn't have to buy one item of black. I had a wardrobe full of it. By the time I became housekeeper I'd just got into the habit.' She paused and beamed at me. 'Into the habit!' she laughed. 'Black. Like a nun. Get it?'

Ho, ho, ho. 'Yes, Mrs O'Dea,' I said with a polite laugh. 'I get it.'

'Well,' she continued, 'I swore never to wear one item of black ever again. All those years in mouldy old black. Ha,

I'd wear a rainbow if I could.'

'You nearly are,' I laughed, pointing to her hat.

Somehow that roll of conversation brought us closer. In spite of her trying to damage our health with her jaw-welding cooking, I was developing a great liking for the old bird. We laughed over our coffee and cream buns. She told me about life in service and I told her about teenage stuff, each of us shocking the other.

Later on she met an old bingo crony. I left them chatting and wandered into a bookshop to have a free look at the magazines. A thin-lipped assistant scowled challengingly at me, so I pretended to be interested in the books.

'I'm looking for some books of poetry,' I said. I knew there wouldn't be so much as a rhyming couplet in the whole shop, but I felt it was necessary to show old thistle-drawers that I was a person of culture who wasn't just in for a free read. Even though I was – in for a free read, I mean. I picked up a tourist booklet about County Kildare and browsed through it. Then, under the heading, *Donnelly's Hollow*, I saw the name Dan Donnelly. Wasn't that the name David had mentioned? The name that his grandfather used to shout, and box the air, when he went ga-ga. But when I read that this Dan Donnelly was a boxer in the last century, I nearly fainted there and then. Could it be that I'd innocently discovered the family roots of David and Eppie?

I paid the £2.50 for the book, which made a bit of a hole in my pocket-money. But, hey, there was a whole ancestral thing in the offing. I couldn't wait to get back to show the others my find.

Of course they reacted with suitable excitement. We went over and over the bit about Dan Donnelly. David had mixed some milkshakes made with real strawberries in

Mrs O'Dea's food processor. He said that in Australia they're big into juice, that they make juice from anything.

'Even brussels sprouts?' I asked.

'If you like that kind of thing,' David replied.

'Thanks, I'll stick with the pretty fruits,' I said, trying to imagine looking dreamily into his eyes over a glass of sprout juice. Even with my poetic outlook, that image didn't quite gel.

We sipped our drinks as we went through the book.

'And he was a boxer,' said David, for the umpteenth time. 'It's no coincidence that Grandpa would box the air and shout "Dan Donnelly", is it?' Imagine, my ancestor could have been a famous boxer. Jeez!'

'But, if he was Donnelly and you're Kelly,' put in Leo. 'How do you make out that you could have come from someone with a different name?'

'Through the female line, you wally,' I said. 'Women have something to offer in this ancestry thing too, you know. The female line could have been Donnelly.'

Leo shrugged. Probably miffed because it was I who'd got things moving.

'Let's go now and show your mum,' I said, thinking I might as well go for the whole ego trip while the going was good.

David shook his head. 'She's gone to Dublin,' he said. 'Won't be back until tonight. Could I borrow the book, Maeve?'

'Keep it,' I said magnanimously. £2.50 was a small price to pay for the privilege of uncovering someone's past. Anyway, they'd be so grateful that they might invite me to Australia.

'Why didn't you go to Dublin with your mother?' asked Leo.

David shrugged. 'I'm happy enough to chill out here with you lot,' he said. 'There are just so many art galleries, museums and scenic spots you can take in before you reach saturation point. Before you folks came along I travelled everywhere with Mum – Sligo, to see Yeats's grave. Though why anyone should get excited about a stone slab over a bunch of bones beats me. We did Cork as well, and Galway. I reckon I've seen enough green fields and ancient ruins to do me a lifetime. No, I'd much rather hang out and have a laugh with you.'

Was it my imagination or was he looking at me when he said that? I smiled at him anyway. The sort of smile that is meaningful and intimate.

Trust Leo to destroy the moment by pointing at me and announcing, 'You have a pink moustache, Maeve. You look like a Teletubby with rabies.'

He stopped when I gave him a don't-mess-with-Maeve look.

David stayed for supper. I was on such a high that I even offered to cook. The sausages, eggs and chips I served were just perfect, naturally.

'We're fresh out of kangaroo steaks and bush tucker,' I joked. David mustn't have heard me because he didn't laugh. Afterwards we watched *Titanic* on video. It wasn't as good as the big screen, you need the surround sound of water gushing and people screaming. The boys did a lot of jeering at what Leo called the slushy parts.

Looking at them, it suddenly struck me: boys take much longer to grow up than girls. Here was I, slightly younger than Jamie, yet I could hold a high-class conversation at a dinner-party. I glanced at Jamie, his long legs sprawled across the floor, a cushion clutched to his chest and a silly grin on his face at something Leo had said. Then he thumped Leo with the cushion, which caused a chain reaction from the other two – just when Kate Winslet was discovering that she didn't love her prat of a husband. Boys are like mongrels, I thought, they make a lot of noise in packs. I sighed for my passing childhood and wondered what it would be like to kiss a man with a moustache.

'Tone it down, you lot,' I said, with great superiority. 'This is a historic film. You're like little kids.'

The three of them looked at me with surprise. Which would have been very satisfying if they hadn't turned on me and thumped me with cushions. Needless to say, I gave as good as I got. It was only when we stopped, exhausted, jaws sore from laughing, that I remembered I was supposed to be mature. Well, tomorrow, maybe.

When we called to David's house next morning, I didn't get the excited reaction I'd expected. In fact David and his mother were very subdued. Maybe Eppie didn't like to think her ancestry circled around a man who boxed with his bare fists for a living. Had I goofed again?

But she smiled and said, 'Thank you for the book, Maeve. It's certainly worth looking into this Dan Donnelly. Perhaps I'll find something on the Net when I get access to it.'

But the way she said it didn't convince me. Something wasn't right.

'Donnelly's Hollow isn't far from here,' said Jamie. 'It's on the Curragh. Grandad took me there when I was a kid. We could cycle there. Montgomerys have some old bikes we could borrow.'

That seemed like a good idea. The bikes were a bit on the creaky side, but they moved okay.

'Mum and I read the article about Donnelly last night,' David said, as we pedalled off. 'She says it's a long shot –

just going on my grandad's senile ramblings. But she'll give it a try.' Then he fell into a morose sort of silence. All his chirpiness seemed to have sunk. I can't bear it when people go weird. First of all I wonder if it has something to do with me, and then I wonder if they've been given really bad news, like a few weeks to live or their cat's been squashed. I couldn't stand it any more, especially when I could see that Jamie and Leo were puzzled too.

'What's wrong, David?' I asked, cycling up beside him.

He looked straight ahead for a moment, as if concentrating heavily on steering his bike. Then he turned to me.

'We've had a threatening letter,' he said.

'What?' I gasped. 'Did you say a *threatening* letter?'

'My Mum and stepdad get those all the time,' said Leo, catching up with us. 'From the bank. "Pay back your loan or else ...".'

'No,' said David. 'Not that sort of threatening letter. Much worse.'

At that we all stopped and dismounted. We wheeled our bikes into the grass of Brigid's big cloak.

'Tell us about it, David,' said Jamie.

David leaned on the handlebars and looked into the distance.

'It was in the letterbox this morning,' he said. 'It had been pushed through. No stamp, so it was some local.'

'Well, what did it say?' I asked impatiently.

'It told us to get out of the country,' replied David. 'Said that there was no room here for people like us and that, if we valued our lives, we should get out pronto.'

'A joke surely,' said Jamie. 'You shouldn't let a silly thing like that upset you. Ignore it.'

David looked at him with an angry expression. 'That's

easy for you, Jamie,' he said. 'But Mum and me ... well ... I don't have to point out to you that we're not exactly shining white.'

I gasped again. 'You mean it was a racist thing?'

David nodded. 'Looks like,' he said.

'Surely not,' put in Jamie. 'The Irish aren't racist, are they?'

I said nothing. From what my dad read aloud from *The Irish Times* some mornings, we seemed to be heading that way.

'Bastards,' Leo swore angrily. 'I wish I could find out who they are and kick their backsides.'

'I still say you should ignore it,' said Jamie. 'Probably just a wimpish prank by some friendless git. Don't let it get to you.'

David shrugged, as if to shake off his cloud of misery.

'I suppose you're right,' he said, getting up on his bike again. 'But Mum was a bit upset.'

We continued on our journey. David seemed to cheer up after sharing his burden with us. It was only a short cycle further to Donnelly's Hollow.

'There it is,' said Leo who, as usual, had raced ahead to be first on the scene.

Below us was a steep hollow with a railed-in monument at the bottom.

'That monument was put up to commemorate Dan Donnelly's fight against an Englishman called George Cooper in 1815,' said David. 'Cooper was so sure he was going to win that he'd booked a feast in a hotel called Robertstown House. But Donnelly beat him and he was mad as hell.'

I was chuffed that he'd read the book I bought.

'What are all those holes in the ground?' asked Leo.

Sure enough, there were two rows of holes which went up one side of the hollow.

'I remember them from when I was here as a kid,' said Jamie. 'They're supposed to be Donnelly's footprints. When he walked up the hill after the fight, people were so delighted that they dug out his footprints to commemorate his win.'

'Deadly,' said Leo.

We ran down into the hollow and tried to walk up the other side in Donnelly's footsteps.

'He must have had long legs,' I panted. 'I can hardly reach from one footprint to the next.'

'He had,' said David. 'And he had long arms as well. He had arms like a gorilla. So the book says.'

'That's true,' laughed Jamie. 'I was telling Grandad that you might be related to Dan Donnelly and he reminded me that he'd taken me to a pub called The Hideout in Kilcullen years ago, when I was little, to see Dan Donnelly's arm. A dirty great arm on display in a glass case. Scared me silly it did. Well, I was only five,' he added. 'It looked like a prop from a horror film. I'd forgotten all about Dan Donnelly until Grandad reminded me, but I sure remembered that arm.'

'That's gross,' I said. I couldn't imagine a pub with a dead man's arm on display. 'Surely people would throw up after a few beers when they'd look up and see a dis-membered arm staring them in the face.'

'Could we go?' exclaimed Leo. 'Could we go and see this arm?'

Jamie shook his head. 'It's not on display there at the moment,' he said. 'I thought we could do that today, but Grandad told me it's been taken away. Look, why don't we go to Newbridge? It's only a few miles from here.'

I was a bit fed up with cycling by now. My bum was sore and my legs felt old. I wished we were going by car. I wished Frank would roll up in a fancy metallic set of wheels with a sun-roof and whisk me away for a candlelight pizza and milkshake. However, I said nothing, just mounted my bike and hoped I wouldn't end up with bulging thighs.

I caught up with David and flashed him a smile, for no particular reason other than keeping Jamie on his toes and reminding David that I was the one who'd brought his historic research this far.

'Interesting bloke, your ancestor,' I said, just before I hit a pot-hole and went into a wobble. 'Hell! Who left that dirty great hole there?' I yelled, which rather spoiled my self-appraisal.

6

Foot in Mouth

After we'd looked in the music shop and bought some goodies for the night, we headed for a coffee shop. As luck would have it, who did we bump into only Frank. It was so unexpected that I hadn't time to get the 'be cool' message to my brain – with the result that I blushed and died right there on the pavement.

'Hello, Maeve,' he said. 'Boys,' he nodded to the lads. 'Just going for a late lunch,' he went on. 'Been holding an auction all morning.'

Wow! There was power in those words.

'Do you have a hammer?' I asked.

'Excuse me?' he smiled at me, one eyebrow raised questioningly. Lovely.

'A hammer,' I went on. 'You know – for banging with when someone bids.'

'Oh,' he laughed. 'I think you mean a gavel, Maeve. Yes, I do.'

I sighed as I envisaged him, moustache wagging as he banged his gavel and sold something of enormous value to some of those types who pretend they're not buying anything at all and just bid by wiping their noses or scratching their heads. I would get so worried if I went to an auction in case I bought some ghastly and useless antique footwarmer or moth-eaten stuffed bear just because I'd sneezed or got itchy.

I rummaged in my mind for something brilliant to say, but there was nothing going on in there except toe-curling confusion. The moment passed because Frank's uncle

Edgar came along. He grinned very friendly-like at us.

'Well, well, who have we here?' he asked. 'Some faces I seem to recognise from the other evening.'

It was Jamie who remembered that neither of them had met David before.

'This is David,' he said. 'He's come from Australia to try and trace his roots.'

Edgar peered at David with interest. 'Good on you, lad,' he said. 'I hope you'll find what you're looking for. Let me know if I can be of any help – point you in the right direction for information and all that.'

'David might be related to Dan Donnelly,' Leo said proudly. 'Did you ever hear of him?'

Edgar laughed. 'Who hasn't!' he said. 'Donnelly was a big hero around these parts many years ago. And you think you might be a descendant of his?' He turned to David.

David shrugged and looked as if he wished Leo hadn't brought up the subject.

'It's just a bit of a hunch,' was all he'd say.

'Did you know that one of his arms used to be on display in The Hideout in Kilcullen?' said Edgar.

Yeah, yeah, we knew all that. I let them drone on while I glanced at Frank and wondered if he'd look good wearing leather and riding a Harley-Davidson, me riding pillion, my hair billowing out behind as we sped across America where all the serious bikers hang out. Then I wondered if he'd ask us to lunch. But all he did was wave as he turned to go down the street with his uncle.

'You should have told them about the threatening letter, David,' said Leo. 'Edgar is connected with the law. They'd know what to do.'

David's face clouded over as he was reminded of that bit of unpleasantness.

'Nah,' he said. 'Anyway, it was probably just a once-off thing.'

'Let's hope so,' said Jamie. 'Maeve?' he went on. 'Are you coming?'

I was still looking back at Frank, noticing the way his dark hair was pleasantly full at the back. 'Yeah,' I sighed.

The coffee was instant stuff and we shared two shaving-foam-filled buns between the four of us. None of us mentioned the letter again.

It had begun to rain when we set off for home. Leo, Jamie and I swore, and David said if they got rain like this in his part of the world they'd celebrate.

'You'd be welcome to it,' I said. 'Your old grandpa knew what he was doing, getting out of this water-logged chunk of turf at the edge of Europe. If you stay here long enough, David, you'll be washed as white as the rest of us... What?' I asked as Leo turned to scowl at me. Did he think I'd purposely made a hurtful remark? Did I have to watch what I'd say from now on just because of one crackpot letter? I hate having to watch what I say because it makes me say what I shouldn't say, if you know what I mean. However, David didn't seem to have picked up any bad vibes; he had his mouth open to let the rain in.

We were on the last stretch of road to the lodge when, as we turned a corner, we were almost driven into the ditch by a car. I should have recognised the screaming gears.

'It's Mrs O'Dea!' I cried, putting out my foot to steady the bike. But I certainly did recognise the passenger peering through the rain-spattered windscreen. 'And old Jack whatisface!'

We watched as the car disappeared around the bend.

'What's she doing with that old geezer in her car?' asked Leo.

'Consorting with the enemy,' said Jamie.

'Maybe he has a gun pointed at her stomach,' I said. 'Maybe he tasted her cooking and is taking her out to shoot her.'

THE BALLAD OF THE DODGY COOK

By Maeve Morris

'Have more pie,' the lady said.
'I'd really like to see you dead.
I'll mourn for you, old weirdy Jack
I have a wardrobe full of black.'
Jack upped and shot her through the heart.
Tore her rainbow dress apart.
'I may be mad,' he chewed and spat.
'But I'd prefer a minced -up rat
Than eat your pies, you wretched cook.
Why don't you get a cookery book?'

We dropped David off at his place and raced home to change out of our wet things. There was a note from Mrs O'Dea telling us she'd had to rush off and that there was lasagne and chips in the freezer.

'I know that,' I said. 'I put them there.' Credit where it's due and all that. 'If it wasn't for me we'd be tucking into glue soup.'

'Yeah, yeah,' said Jamie, as he ran upstairs two at a time.

I looked at Leo and shrugged. It wasn't like Jamie to be so dismissive. Boys, I thought. So childish.

Later in the afternoon Mrs O'Dea came back.

'We saw you,' said Leo, getting straight to the point. 'You had that old Jack in the car with you.' He stopped, waiting for Mrs O'Dea to give an account of herself.

But all she said was, 'That's right. Did you manage to cook for yourselves?' and disappeared into her room. When she emerged half an hour later, she was dressed as if for a siege. Over her windcheater she was wearing a floppy cardigan, woollen socks peeked from above her wellies, and the rainbow hat was firmly pulled over her ears.

'Mrs O'Dea, it's lashing rain, but it's still only late summer,' I said. 'Are you going to the North Pole?'

She laughed as she fished a powerful lamp from a kitchen cupboard.

'I have to go out for a while,' she said. 'I'll probably be very late back. Will you do your own supper?'

'Sure,' said Jamie. Again we waited for some explanation but, with a wave, she was gone.

'What on earth is she up to?' I asked.

'Looks like we're not going to be let in on the secret,' said Jamie.

'Maybe she's gone hunting for some wild creatures to make a stew,' I went on. 'Squirrel surprise or curried fox. That woman should be issued with a government health warning. Anyway, one of you can do supper. I did it last night. And I don't mean boiled sausages à la Boy Scouts.'

Jamie stuck out his jaw with a sort of grim determination. 'I'll do it,' he said. 'I'm a fair cook.'

'What?' I teased. 'Do you mean to say that you take over at home when it's cook's day off?' That was a good-humoured reference to Jamie's London lifestyle. His parents were both into big careers with mega bucks. But he didn't smile. He just went to the fridge and began pulling things about.

'Come on, Leo,' he said. 'Lend a hand.'

I supposed he was saving me from any trouble. That, or he was trying to prove something. Still, I felt a bit miffed as I plonked on the sofa.

He rustled up a pretty nifty trough of nosh. There were rashers, sausages and burgers for himself and me, a decent looking omelette for veggie Leo, and a plate of floury potatoes.

'This is good,' I said, tucking in. 'Full of cholesterol, of course,' I added, just so that he wouldn't get a swelled head. 'A heart-stopping meal.'

'Oh, shut up, Maeve,' said Leo.

I looked at Jamie. He was concentrating on cutting his burger. There was an awkward silence. The sort of tense silence you get when you know someone in the group is fed up and you don't know why.

'Well, you two are a barrel of laughs,' I said eventually. 'I hope David comes soon. I could do with a bit of company.'

David did come. He had a video which his mother had brought from town. He said she was going to stay in Athlone and then go to Clonmacnoise early in the morning.

'Doesn't she know it's raining?' I asked.

'That doesn't worry Mum,' replied David. 'She says we didn't come here for the weather and it certainly won't stop her seeing whatever it is she wants to see.'

'I know Clonmacnoise,' I said, delighted to know at least one historic site. 'A place where monks used to carve crosses and things. A lot of old stone. You'd be much better off with us, David.'

But I could see that he couldn't decide whether to go with her or stay with us.

'Stay, David,' I said, flapping the old eyelashes a bit. 'We'd like you to stay with us.' I looked at Jamie to catch his reaction, but he'd begun to fiddle with the video.

It was a boring video, about car chases and stupid explosions. I spent a lot of time tapping my feet and groaning loudly.

When it was over, we sat on the floor. The rain was beating a patter on the windows. 'Candles!' I exclaimed. 'This sort of dreariness is just crying out for candles.' I had seen some bundles earlier on Mrs O'Dea's dresser. I scattered about six of them around the room and turned out the main light.

'There,' I said. 'Isn't that romantic?'

Leo snorted. 'Like a wake,' he said.

'Tell us, David,' I said, sitting cross-legged on the furry rug, 'tell us about Australia.'

'Tell you what?' asked David. 'It's big, it's hot, it's a good place to live.'

'Ah, come on,' I insisted. 'Tell us about ... about your people.'

'The Aborigines, you mean?'

I nodded.

He laughed a sort of bitter laugh. 'It's a short story,' he said. 'They lived with the land for centuries.'

'What do you mean "with"?' asked Leo.

'Just that,' replied David. 'They never claimed to own the land, they lived in harmony with it, moving about from place to place. Then the conquering heroes arrived with boat-loads of prisoners to dump, took over the land and pushed the Aboriginal people farther and farther into the desert. They even took to hunting them for sport. Treated them like animals.'

'Never,' I gasped. This was heavy. I'd only wanted to hear about walkabouts, koalas and wallabies, didgeridoo music and big sheep-shearers with bouncy corks on their hats.

'Oh yes,' went on David. 'The settlers even tried to wipe out the Aborigines completely by taking children forcibly from their families, bringing them up like white kids and marrying them to white partners so that Aboriginal blood would gradually disappear.'

'But that's awful,' I said. 'What a cruel time the last century must have been.'

'Last century?' said David. 'They were doing that in my own mother's generation, for crissake! She knew of people from her own area whose children were taken away.'

'But that's awful,' I said again. 'Was that what happened to your grandmother, the one who fell off the horse?'

'No,' David answered. 'That was a love match. My grandad wasn't racist.'

'Who were they, these settlers who came and took the land?' asked Leo.

David fiddled with the tassles that hung from the sofa and shrugged his shoulders.

'Look, it was a long time ago,' he said. 'What does it matter? We shouldn't be harbouring grudges from the past, that's the stupid stuff that causes wars. Forget it, eh?'

Without stopping to think, I leapt in with my motor-mouth in top gear.

'British, weren't they? But they did the same to us,' I cried. 'For hundreds of years they tried to put us down, but they got their comeuppance. We sent them running. Ha!'

The deathly silence was broken only by the patter of raindrops. I glanced at Jamie and, too late, realised my foot was firmly planted in my mouth. 'I mean ... ,' I began.

'I know what you meant, Maeve,' said Jamie evenly. 'Everything is cut and dried for you, isn't it? Maeve is right and the rest of the world is wrong. Here we are, at the turn

of the millennium and you're just dying to take a shot at me because of who I am. You're just as bad as all those troublemakers in Ulster who keep old wars stoked up instead of getting on with life.'

He leaned closer to me, his eyes so angry that they truly scared the daylights out of me. This was a Jamie I didn't know and he was freaking me out.

'I'm not ...' I stammered.

'Yes, you are,' he went on. 'Look at us, the four of us. We're the next generation. We've been doing just fine, until all of this came up. Now, suddenly, I'm the bad guy because I belong to a country with a conquering past. I had nothing to do with any of it, any more than you had anything to do with whatever your ancestors did – after all some of your lot went out there too. But, don't worry, I'll take myself away from your company and you can ...'

'Hold on there, mates,' put in David. 'Let's not have this blow up in our faces. Jamie is right. It's nothing to do with us. Come on, forget it.'

But Jamie had got up and was leaving the room. I ran after him, I couldn't leave things like this.

'Jamie,' I called as he started up the stairs. 'I didn't mean it. I really didn't.'

He turned and looked down at me. 'No, of course you didn't,' he said. 'Any more than you meant the remarks about the dinner I cooked, or any other rudeness that spills from that mouth of yours. I suppose you didn't mean it either when you ignored me at Montgomerys the other night, chatting like a chimp to Frank Jellet and then throwing words like, "culture", at me. And then flirting with David and looking to see if I noticed. If you were trying to make me jealous, get real, Maeve. I go to a mixed school. There are girls in my year who would knock you sideways with intelligence and looks. You're ... you're pathetic.'

Then he was gone, with a slam of his bedroom door.

I have never felt so deflated and defeated in my whole life. I hated myself.

7

Jack

I'm not normally given to weepy moments. I've always held that weeping is for wimpy types with candy-floss for brains. But, that night I snivelled through at least two packets of tissues and the sleeves of my pyjamas. All this time, with my grand ideas about maturing, Jamie was the one who'd grown up. I was the one behaving like a dumbo.

If only I could rub out the early part of this night; no, if only I could rub out the start of this holiday and begin again. I'd be so cool and grown-up. I wouldn't go getting a crush on a man old enough to have a job and a hairy upper lip. I'd be nice to Jamie and monitor everything I'd say *before* opening my mouth. I'd make David and his mother think I was a wonderful human being, and I'd make Mr McLaren see me as a brilliant companion for his grandson.

I blew my nose for the umpteenth time. My heart leapt when there was a tap on the door. I wiped my face on the sheet, sure that it was Jamie come to apologise.

But it was only Leo.

'Oh, it's you,' I muttered.

He sat on the edge of the bed and, looking at me with a worried expression, said, 'Are you all right?'

'Huh, Leo, you don't think I'd let that creep upset me, do you? What do you think I am?'

Leo got up. 'Okay,' he said, making for the door. 'I just thought I'd ask.'

'No, wait, Leo,' I said in a softer voice. 'I'm not all right. I'm in bits here.' He paused and then came back. 'I made a right eejit of myself, didn't I?' I continued.

'Well ...' he began, and got stuck.

'You don't have to be polite,' I went on. 'I know I ruined everything. Am I really as bad as I think I might be, Leo?'

He turned this one over in his mind for a moment. Then he shook his head.

'Sometimes you say things,' he said. 'But you're okay. Jamie will come round, you'll see. He knows you didn't really mean any harm. I think.'

'Where is he now?' I asked.

'He's gone to the house. Says he's going to stay there.'

'Oh, no,' I groaned. 'And David?'

'Went home. Said he'd probably go to Clonmacnoise with his mother after all.'

'Oh, cripes, Leo. I've gone and done it now, haven't I? I've broken up our brilliant group.'

Leo shrugged. 'I'm still here,' he said. 'I'll hang out with you tomorrow.'

That was Leo, always so calm about everything. Just like his mother. The house could fall down around Aunt Brid's ears and she'd just carry on regardless. Why couldn't I have inherited that trait? Where was I when the good genes were being distributed in our family? Out to lunch?

I looked at him through my puffy eyes. 'You're all right, kid,' I said, with a pathetic smile. 'Thanks for coming in.'

'Don't be crying, Maeve,' said Leo, as the waterworks in my eyes went into overflow again. 'It scares me to see you crying. You're not the type.'

'Oh yeah?' I sniffed. 'And what type am I?'

Leo wrinkled his nose in thought. 'You're, well, you're you,' he said.

I sighed. 'That's my problem, Leo, being me.'

'Now you're going soft in the head,' said Leo, helpfully.

'Look, sleep on it. You'll be okay in the morning. Things will work out.'

'You really think so?' I asked.

Leo looked back at me from the door. 'Yeah, they will. Your eyes and nose are all red,' he went on, with a grin. 'You look like someone from Comic Relief.'

That bit of normality repaired some of the broken-down cells in my chemical make-up.

It suddenly occurred to me that, like the women poets who had tuberculosis and the vapours, I now had my very own tragic chunk of life to stir me into great poetry.

THE TRAGIC LOVE

By Maeve Morris

My love has gone and left me weeping.
Into my heart, cold ice is creeping.
I wish he'd come, my dearest bloke,
And tell me that it's all a joke.
And though a man with hairy lip
Might take me off on a big ship,
It's Jamie who's my shining light.
Why did we have that cruddy fight?

The next morning Mrs O'Dea reacted with surprise when Leo told her that Jamie had gone to stay at Montgomerys.

'Had a row, had you?' she asked.

Leo and I looked at one another sheepishly. 'Sort of,' said Leo.

Mrs O'Dea laughed. 'Sometimes we need the odd tiff to clear the air,' she said.

Clear the air? This so-called tiff had cleared a whole friendship right out of orbit.

'How did it start?' she asked.

I did the decent thing and came clean. 'I think it might have been something I said,' I muttered.

Mrs O'Dea laughed. 'I could have guessed,' she said. She leaned towards me and patted my hand. 'You remind me of myself when I was your age several life-times ago.'

Huh? I thought (but didn't say, mind you). Black clothes? Black *stockings*? Knowing your place? Bowing to authority? Scrubbing fireplaces and starching big knickers? I think not!

However, something happened which knocked all thoughts of the row off our minds.

As Leo and I walked past David's house later in the morning, we were appalled to see graffiti in big red letters scrawled on the gable end: 'Go back where you belong'. Underneath it was a crude drawing of a skull.

'Jeez, Leo,' I gasped. 'Someone has it in for David and his mother. I wonder have they seen it yet?'

But then we remembered that they'd gone to Athlone the previous evening

'They'll be very upset,' said Leo.

'Look,' I said. 'Let's clean it off, you and me. That way they'll never know. We can't let them see this.'

We headed back to the lodge at top speed. Mrs O'Dea had gone out, but we knew where she kept J-cloths and cleaning stuff. As we rubbed, I kept glancing towards the road to see if Jamie might come looking for us.

'You're looking out for him, aren't you?' said Leo eventually. 'Jamie. You're hoping he'll come by.'

'Who?' I said. 'You must be joking. I wouldn't give that stuck-up creep a second glance. Looking out for him? Yeah, like I'm hoping Count Dracula will drop by for a nip at my neck.'

By the time we'd finished, there were just some reddish stains left, nobody would ever know there had been graffiti there. We stretched ourselves, admired our work and decided we needed sustenance of the chocolate-biscuit kind. When we got back to the house, there was a light on Mrs O'Dea's answering machine.

'That could be from your folks or mine,' I said. 'Might even be urgent. They might have won the lottery and need our help to decide what to do with all the money.'

'Don't touch it, Maeve,' said Leo. 'That's none of our business.'

'Well, can't do any harm,' I said. 'She'll never know.'

I pressed the playback switch. At first there were some clicking noises, as if the person leaving the message didn't quite know what to do. Then a voice came on. An old voice. A man.

'Mai,' he said, in an anxious sort of tone. 'I heard them again after you left last night. They're driving me mad, Mai. I've told the gardai again, but I know they think I'm just imagining it. I don't know what to do. What should I do, Mai?'

Leo and I looked at one another with dismay. 'What was that all about?' asked Leo.

'Beats me,' I replied. 'But it sounds weird. I suppose it's that crazy old Jack. He's obviously gone loopy, just as everyone says.'

'What do you suppose he heard?' said Leo.

'Voices,' I answered.

'Voices?'

'Yes. The voices of aliens come to abduct him and do experiments on him. They'll put microchips in his head, if they haven't already done so, and give him a Kalashnikov so that he can really shift trespassers off his land. Then they'll set up an alien lab in his house and take over the world.'

'Oh, give over,' laughed Leo. 'Put that tape back to the start and let's get something to eat. We can have it in the back garden.'

The tea and biscuits didn't taste the same. Not without the others. And the afternoon ahead loomed long and boring. Until, that is, there was a frantic ringing on the doorbell. Could it be Jamie? My heart started to thump, but it went back to its usual beat when I realised that Jamie wouldn't ring. He'd have come around the back like always. Together, Leo and I went around the side of the house which led to the front of the lodge. We both recoiled when we saw who the visitor was.

For a moment we gaped at old Jack and he gaped at us. Then his face became thunderous.

'You!' he roared. 'What are you doing hanging around here? Is it not enough that you're pestering me, but you have to come scaring this good lady as well! I have you now, ye dangerous little criminals. There's no getting away now.' He lunged at us, moving fast for such a crochety old geezer. Leo and I scarpered back into the garden – a garden enclosed by a high wall. We were trapped, with a manic geriatric on our heels. As we shrank against an ivied wall, I hoped he wasn't about to pull a shotgun from under his long coat.

'We're staying with Mrs O'Dea!' I shouted, when I found my voice. 'We're her guests.'

'Liars!' he roared. 'Where's the rest of your gang? Out terrorising someone else? I'll have you flung into jail, the lot of you.'

'Look, mister,' I said, as reasonably as I could, but with a certain amount of panic creeping in – I'd never had to

deal with a madman before, especially an old one. 'I don't know who you think we are, but we're staying with Mrs O'Dea.'

He made another lunge, but we were too quick for him. I glanced towards the path that led to the front of the house. Would we ever make it? Well, one of us would. Normally that would be me, but then I remembered how Leo had come to check on my tragic ego last night, so I gave him a push and got between him and Doctor Death.

'Run, Leo!' I shouted. 'Get help.'

Now, here I was, extra tragic and stuck in a trap with a loopy old man who thought I belonged to some gang. Right now I wished I had a gang here. Any gang.

'Just tell me who you are and why you're pestering me,' said the old man. 'For the past two weeks now. Why?'

'What makes you think it's us?' I asked.

'Voices,' he said. 'I know your voices. Young voices. Why are you doing it? And don't think you'll get past me,' he added as my eyes darted around for somewhere to run. 'I'll not let you go until you tell me.'

There was no reasoning with this character. Was this it? Was I not even going to get time to do the growing-up bit that I'd promised myself last night? Would I die without anyone finding out that I could really be as sophisticated as those girls in Jamie's school?

'Hey!' a cry rang out. I could have wept again, this time for joy, when I saw Leo run in accompanied by Jamie. 'Hey!' Jamie called out again.

The old man turned, but I was too petrified to move.

'It's all right, Mister,' said Jamie, as if he was talking to a difficult horse. 'We're friends of Mrs O'Dea. We're staying with her.'

The old man looked confused for a moment. Then I could see the anger rise in his face again. I should have run when I had the chance. However, the situation was saved when Mrs O'Dea herself appeared.

'What's going on?' she called. 'Jack, is that you? I've just been to your place. I got your phone message earlier this morning. What's all this?'

I let out a sigh of relief. Life seemed suddenly very precious. Mrs O'Dea gently led Jack into the house. When I saw his pathetic figure from the back, all bony and baggy clad, I wondered what I had been afraid of. But then I remembered the anger in his face and realised he was as mad as a baboon in a thistle bed.

'Are you all right, Maeve?' Leo was running towards me.

I nodded and slid to the grass, on account of my knees suddenly being deprived of that adrenalin I already spoke of. 'I'm fine,' I said. 'Just give me a minute.'

Jamie hung around in the background. What should I do? Get up and sweep haughtily into the house? Turn catatonic and pretend he wasn't there? Curl up and die? Scream blue murder at him for the awful things he said to me? I did none of these things, because he came and stood over me.

'Did he hit you?' he asked.

'He did not,' I replied. 'He wouldn't dare mess with me, the old goat. Thought I belonged to some gang that he says is terrorising him. Me? Do I look like some Mafia babe? Or someone who mugs ould fellas?' My mouth had forgotten and gone right ahead without my having time to cool it. I glanced up at Jamie to see was he reacting like he did last night. But he was smiling.

'Come on,' he said, holding out his hand to help me up. 'Let's get this sorted out.'

We didn't say anything as we made our way towards the house, but I was comfortable in the knowledge that, without big cringing apologies and embarrassingly cosmetic declarations of undying friendship, things would smooth over. It only took my life-and-death situation to patch the gap created by angry words. Still, I vowed, I'd try very hard to match those slick bimbos in his school. And I certainly wouldn't try to make him jealous in future, at least not so loudly.

Jack was sitting in an armchair, like a scarecrow in an old coat. Mrs O'Dea was pouring whiskey into a glass. She turned when she saw us.

'Come in, children,' she said. 'I was just telling Mr Jack who you are. Sit down and I'll tell you what's been happening.'

We looked at one another a bit uncertainly. Whatever

was churning this man's brain, we didn't really want to know.

'Sit down,' commanded Mrs O'Dea. We sat, keeping out of range of bony fingers or concealed shotguns. 'This is Mr Jack Horton,' she went on, pouring a tipple for herself as well. 'He lives in Tubbermore House, which goes back to the seventeen hundreds and was once the finest house for miles around, with racing stables that were second to none.'

'That's nice,' I said. Now that we'd been established as honest citizens, maybe me and the boys could go.

'Not so nice,' said Mrs O'Dea, looking sympathetically at the old man, whose colour was beginning to return. 'Like most big houses, it ran into difficulties. But Mr Jack is holding on to his house. He's leased the land ...'

'But Tubbermore House will hold my family name until I die,' put in Mr Jack. 'I'll not sell out. No matter what, I'm not selling out.'

'But it seems that someone wants him out,' said Mrs O'Dea. 'For the past couple of weeks there have been strange goings-on at the house.'

'Voices,' said Jack. 'Children's voices, laughing and jeering.' He paused and rubbed his forehead as if to brush away some awful anxiety. 'It's not people, Mai,' he went on quietly. 'It's ghosts. You heard them yourself.'

I nudged Leo in an attempt to share my thought that, not alone was this a garrulous old fogey, but he was also wired to the moon. Ghosts? Get real!

'Ah, get away with you,' said Mrs O'Dea. 'Ghosts me eye! There's no such thing, Jack. It's some crowd with nothing better to do. The gardai have done all they could,' she went on, looking over at the three of us. 'Mr Jack has rung them every evening since all of this started, but the torment never happens when they're around. Even Edgar Jellett, who's a good friend, brought a garda out once or twice at night, but nothing happened. Short of posting someone round the clock, they can't do any more. It's got that they don't believe us, and who could blame them?' she went on, patting the old man's skeletal knee.

'They think I'm just a fanciful old man,' said Jack, with a wry smile. 'But I'll stay put, ghosts or no ghosts.'

Mrs O'Dea was shaking her head. 'Kids up to no good, Jack,' she said gently. 'If I could catch them I'd leather them.'

Now I saw this pathetic old man for what he really was. Garrulous fogey or not, nobody had the right to scare an old man in his own home. No wonder the poor codger had reacted when he saw the four of us charging up to his house. If it had been me, I'd have shot each of us dead and fed the bodies to the dogs. Still, I had to get my spoke in.

'Well, you can't go thinking that *every* young person is out to get you,' I muttered. 'Whatever about that first time when we were on your land, you'd no right to attack us here. We're not all hooligans, you know,' I added with just enough bitterness to set the record straight. 'Our people are very high up.'

There was a muffled snort from Leo, with his hand clamped over his mouth.

Mrs O'Dea made a soothing gesture with the hand that wasn't holding the whiskey glass. 'Hush, dear,' she said. 'Please understand that Mr Jack is going through ...'

'It's all right, Mai,' put in the old man. He looked at me. I wondered was it what I'd said that was making the vein in his forehead throb, and if he dropped dead because of it, would I be guilty? 'I'm really sorry, children,' he went on softly. 'What can I say? Whoever is doing this is making me lose my reason. I just hope Mai is right, that it *is* people who are doing it.'

'That's awful,' I said. 'Can't you set a trap for them?'

'That's the strange bit,' said Mrs O'Dea. 'We hear the voices, but when we go to where we hear them, they start laughing from another part of the house.'

'Dead spooky,' said Leo.

I had to agree. And the hairs on the back of my neck thought so too, because they'd risen to the thought.

'And only the two of you have heard them?' asked Jamie.

Mrs O'Dea nodded. 'Just us,' she said. 'So you can see why the gardai groan whenever Mr Jack or I phone them. They think we're just a pair of paranoid old fools. I hate those kids for their cruelty. I really hate them. You mustn't let them get to you, Jack.'

'Whatever they are,' said Jack. 'They're driving me mad.'

'Is there nobody who would move into the house and live with you?' I asked. 'Some relation?'

'Mr Jack is the last of his line,' said Mrs O'Dea, patting his knee again. I was amused at the old-fashioned way she called him 'Mister Jack' to us and just plain 'Jack' when she was talking to him directly. Old habits die hard. 'And his foolish pride is keeping him from doing something to make his old age comfortable,' she went on. 'How many times have I asked you to sell the whole dreary lot and move in here with me, you stubborn old mule?'

Jack drained the last of his whiskey and stood up. 'I'd better be getting back,' he said. 'There's a man coming to buy timber.' He looked at Jamie, Leo and me in turn. 'Sorry about my outburst,' he went on. 'But you see how

I'm in a bit of a state at the moment. I'm not such a bad sort really,' he added with a smile that transformed his face from Death on a bad hair day to, well, Death with a bowl of cherries. 'When this business is sorted out you must come and have tea at Tubbermore House.'

He refused Mrs O'Dea's offer of a lift home. Wise man.

'The walk will keep my bones from seizing up,' he said.

When he was gone, we all started talking at once.

'What do you think, Mrs O'Dea?' asked Jamie, when he could get a word in.

Mrs O'Dea sighed and drained her glass before putting away the whiskey and taking the glasses into the kitchen. We followed her and sat around the table.

'I don't know what to think,' she said. 'I don't believe in all that phantom stuff. And yet ...' she broke off and concentrated on testing the water from the hot tap.

'And yet what?' I prompted.

She shrugged and then turned to face us. 'I'd never admit to Mr Jack that it might be some sort of restless spirits,' she said. 'I'm sure that would give him a heart attack. That's why I keep insisting that it's kids, at least that keeps it at human level. But I get this chilled feeling in my bones when I hear those voices, here one minute, in another room the next. I stayed with him until three o'clock this morning and it was as much as I could do not to run from that house. Poor Mr Jack, so proud. And he refuses to tell anyone else. Made me promise not to say a word to anyone, except for Edgar and the gardai. Edgar has been so good. He searched high and low and checked all the locks. But there's not much more he can do either. We go back years and years, Mr Jack and me,' she went on, rinsing the glasses. 'He used to come to the house above to play chess with old Mr Montgomery, in the days when I was housekeeper. Mr Jack was always a reclusive man. Not one for social gatherings, was Jack. Even when he would come to some dinner-party or other, he'd end up in my little sitting-room, just chatting.'

'Didn't he marry?' I asked, ever on the look-out for a slice of romance – purely for poetic research, you understand.

Mrs O'Dea shook her head. 'There was a girl once,' she said. 'Back in the nineteen-fifties.' She breathed on the glasses as she polished them with a clean tea-towel.

'What happened?' I asked.

'She got polio and died,' she replied. 'He was heart-broken. But he never had another romantic attachment after that.'

'Oh, that's just so sad,' I whispered. 'I hate sad stories.'

Mrs O'Dea laughed. 'Oh, Mr Jack is happy in his own old way,' she said. Her face darkened. 'At least he was up to now. I wish I knew what to do. I know if I tell the gardai again, they'll throw up their hands. That's the downside of being old, you see. People think you imagine things in your dotage.'

'Could we help, do you think?' asked Jamie. 'If we went along tonight and heard all these voices, someone might believe us.'

'That's right,' agreed Leo. 'And if they are kids, we could chase them.'

Mrs O'Dea looked doubtful. 'I don't know,' she began.

'The lads are right,' I put in. 'We'd catch them and punch the daylights out of them.'

'Well, not so much that,' said Jamie. 'But at least we could find out what's going on.'

'D'ye think so?' asked Mrs O'Dea.

We nodded. And so it was settled. That night we'd go

with Mrs O'Dea to Tubbermore House, either to lay
Jack's ghost, or else thump a crowd of prats.

THE HEARTBROKEN HERMIT

By Maeve Morris

The old man lived all by himself.
A loner he, upon the shelf.
At night he grieved for his dead love
Whose spirit gazed down from above.
'My dearest dear,' he fondly cried.
'I really wish you hadn't died
And left me here in this old house
To weep and be a grumpy grouse.'
But voices came and drove him mad,
(This poem's really much too sad).

8

Tubbermore House

As we walked down the road towards the small shop that was laughingly called 'The Hypermarket', we were talking about Jack and arguing about whether the voices might be ghosts or sicko creeps. I was plugging for the ghosts myself. That's what comes of being a very creative person; you tend to go with the spiritual. That's why a lot of poets and painters went mad, but that's a risk you have to take when you assume the mantle of greatness.

'Hi!' someone shouted behind us.

'It's David,' said Leo.

Sure enough, so it was. He was panting as he caught up with us.

'Did you have a nice time in Clonmacnoise?' I asked, extra cheerfully, so that he'd know that yesterday's war was history. 'Did you get the smell of dead monks?'

'It was okay,' he gasped, out of breath from chasing after us. 'Lots of old stuff. Athlone was good too. We went to see a movie last night.' He took a paper from his pocket.

'We've had another one,' he said.

'Another what?' asked Leo.

'A threatening letter, is it?' put in Jamie.

David nodded and handed it to him. We craned over Jamie's shoulder to read it.

'Go now,' it read. 'Get back to your own country ...'

'Racist prats!' I exclaimed.

... 'Your mother was killed by a horse, so could your boy. Accidents can happen. Be warned.'

'That's awful, David,' said Jamie, folding up the letter

and handing it back. 'How did they know that? About your grandmother, I mean. It's weird.'

'I know,' agreed David. 'Who could possibly have known that? That's what makes it all the more scary. You're the only people who know all that stuff.'

A sudden thought occurred to me that made me turn away to hide a guilty blush. I remembered how I'd blabbed about David and his mother to Frank that night at the dinner. Could Frank possibly have had anything to do with this? No, never. Why on earth would Frank wish any harm to David and Eppie? The thought was too ludicrous. No, this was some person or persons unknown, as they say on *Crimewatch*. However, I didn't say anything to the boys.

'But why would anyone wish harm to you and your mother?' asked Leo.

David shrugged. 'Dunno, mate,' he said. 'But Mum is seriously considering chucking it in and going home.'

'But that would be giving in to them!' I said. 'Are you going to give these ... these rotten sods the satisfaction of running you out?'

David shrugged again. 'Easy for you to say, Maeve,' he replied. 'But it's scary when you're at the receiving end.'

'I don't think I like this part of the country,' I went on. 'Between Jack's voices and now this, I get the feeling that we're in hostile territory.'

'What's this about voices?' asked David, thrusting the letter into his pocket.

And so we told him about the antics of the morning. It was then I remembered the graffiti that Leo and I had cleaned away. I was about to blurt it out when Leo caught my eye and shook his head. He knew what I was going to say and stopped me mid-breath. He was quite right. There was enough going on without adding that.

The shop was full when we got there. That meant that there were three people at the counter. We were surprised to see that Edgar was one of them. He turned his beaming face on us as he put the tobacco he'd just bought into his pocket.

'Hello, young folks,' he said, smiling.

'Hello, Mr Jellett.'

'Oh, call me Edgar,' he laughed. 'Mister sounds so stuffy. I've just been up to Montgomerys on business,' he went on. 'I was chatting with your grandad, young man,' he nodded to Jamie. 'He certainly knows his horses.'

Jamie smiled politely, as Jamie does. 'He's been breeding them for years,' he said.

'My dad smokes that brand,' I said, pointing to the pocket with the tobacco in it. Just to show that my folks had a touch of class too. Well, just a bit.

Edgar laughed. 'A man of impeccable taste,' he said. 'And lucky to have a daughter like you. All I have are boys. Three of the rowdiest youngsters you could imagine. In fact there's a party for the oldest tomorrow. He'll be eight. Why don't you four come along? It will be noisy, but there will be plenty of goodies. You could help organise games of football. How about it?'

We looked at one another to see who would take on the task of decision maker.

'Great,' said Jamie. 'We'd be delighted, wouldn't we?' He turned to us three. We nodded and muttered our thanks.

'Good,' said Edgar. 'At two then, okay?' And he was gone.

'What did you want to agree to that for?' I asked, selecting my choice of chocolate. 'Crummy kids. Well, I suppose at least we'll get some decent nosh.'

'Would you like to come with us tonight, David?' asked Jamie, when we went outside. 'The more the better.'

David concentrated on peeling the paper off his Yorkie before replying.

'I suppose so,' he said. 'But what will I tell my ma? I don't think she'd be thrilled with me putting myself in some sort of danger. Not with these letters we've been getting.'

'Tell her you're dossing down with us for the night,' I said. 'That's not really a lie, just a slight bending of the truth.'

David grinned. 'Okay, you're on,' he said.

Well, at least it would take his mind off racist letters, I thought.

'It's doing my head in,' I said. 'All this heavy stuff – spooks and racist threats – is giving me the creeps. My brain is picking up vibes of paranoia.'

I could see that both Jamie and Leo had smart remarks on the tips of their tongues. But neither of them said anything. Last night's row was still only cooling down and nobody wanted to say anything that would spark it off again. Still, I can't stand a cagey atmosphere. 'I suppose one of you heroes was going to say that my brain is lucky if it picks up vibes of any sort,' I said, just to get it out of the way.

Jamie laughed. That was good.

Like a bunch of undercover cops on a stake-out, we got ready for our vigil in Jack's house.

'Dress warmly,' said Mrs O'Dea. 'It's a draughty old house, even in summer.'

She had on her usual multi-coloured layers. She lent David one of her floppy sweaters and a woolly hat.

'You look like a fluffy Action Man,' I giggled.

He laughed and pointed at my combats. 'And you look like a stick insect with mucky legs,' he said. I thought that was a bit over the top. I'd had to fight hard to get those combats. Which is very fitting, if you think about it.

'Everybody ready?' asked Mrs O'Dea.

We chugged up the pot-holed avenue to Tubbermore House. It looked big and spooky in the moonlight. Some of the downstairs lights were on. I couldn't quite believe that we were calmly doing this. It was like that feeling you get on a ghost train, just before the doors yawn open. Except that here it was the front door that opened and this was for real. Jack's frail form was silhouetted against the light. He was wearing a woolly cardy that hung from his thin shoulders. What was it with old people, I wondered, that they had to wrap themselves in the sloppiest of gear? Maybe that was what this was all about. Some restless spirits with good taste who couldn't stand sloppy, hairy clothes and came back to banish them from knitting needles everywhere.

'I've brought extra hands,' said Mrs O'Dea, unloading the basket of doorstep sandwiches and granite buns she'd prepared against the long night.

'I thought you might,' said Jack, opening the door wider to admit us. We gasped in awe. Stuffed animal heads hung like sentries over the four doors that led off the big hall. Gross monstrosities that should have been given a decent burial years ago. Better still, the poor creatures should have been allowed to die of natural causes while their heads were still attached to their bodies.

A long passage on one side led to what was obviously the kitchen because there was a lingering smell of cooking. A majestic staircase, like in those musicals where someone dances down a load of steps with men in top hats, led

upstairs. The wall beside the staircase was lined with portraits and dreary landscapes.

'Wow!' I said. 'Cool hall.'

'Come down to the kitchen,' said Jack. 'It's much warmer there.'

I made a mental note to educate these old people about modern language.

'Come on, David,' called Mrs O'Dea.

David was peering at a painting.

'Interesting picture,' he said.

'My mother painted that,' said Jack, with a mixture of sadness and pride. 'It's actually a folly. Many follies were built during the famine.'

'Folly?' David looked puzzled.

'Means something strange or foolish,' laughed Mrs O'Dea. 'Only built to give employment.'

We trooped after Jack. The kitchen was obviously where he spent most of his time. It had what my da would call a 'lived in' look, and what my mother would call a right mess. There were newspapers piled on chairs, a table that looked like it was never cleared, an armchair that looked as if it had come straight off the set of *Father Ted*, and an Aga with a big kettle steaming on it. A ginger cat jumped from one of the chairs and came over to purr at us. I stooped to rub him and he purred even more loudly and fondled my hand.

'Anything happen yet, Jack?' asked Mrs O'Dea, putting the sandwiches on a plate.

He shook his head. 'Bit early yet,' he said. 'It's always after midnight when they start, the wretches.' He sighed and eased himself into the grubby armchair. Mrs O'Dea pulled the faded curtains across the big Georgian windows to shut out the night. 'All we can do is wait,' she said.

We made ourselves comfortable. Jack produced a jug of orange juice from the antiquarian fridge. It was ghastly. The sort of orange juice that makes your throat turn to acid.

We chatted. Mostly it was us listening to Jack and Mrs O'Dea talking about the old days when the house was full of life. It was like a history lesson, only these two old people *were* the history. We looked at ancient photos of elegant women with waists and big hats posing with funny shaped tennis racquets. Men in Sherlock Holmes hats sat stiffly and proudly in the sort of cars you'd see in cartoons. But it was the photos of Jack that took my breath away. He was a hunk, with black hair and a square jaw. He reminded me of someone, probably some pre-historic film idol I'd seen in one of Dad's old movie magazines. When you've seen one moustachioed swashbuckler with oily hair and American teeth, you've seen them all. I stole a glance at him and thought what a weird sense of humour God must have had when he created old age. No wonder he opted out of earthly life when he was thirty-three.

'Who is this, riding bareback?' asked David, peering at a brown photo of a young man on horseback.

'He was my uncle,' said Jack. 'My mother's brother. Horses were a huge part of our background.'

'I love horses,' said David, still peering at the photo. 'I've ridden bareback in the bush.'

'The African bush ...?' began Jack. I supposed it was a reasonable question because we hadn't told him that David was from Australia. But I felt it was a typical lumping together of all dark-skinned people as African. However, before I could launch into putting the racial perspective right, we heard the first cackle of laughter. My heart crossed over to the other side of my rib-cage. It was a horrible sound. Not horrible as a sound, but horrible because it was so much out of context. An old Georgian house at midnight is not the place to hear childish laughter. Mrs O'Dea sat up straight.

'That sounds like it's coming from the library,' she said, jerking her bones into action. We followed her down the hall to a large, panelled door. She stood for a moment and put her finger to her lips. We froze. I thanked my stars that we were all together; if I'd been on my own I'd have passed away by now. Which made me realise what old Jack must have been going through. Me? I'd have *given* the cruddy house away, packed a toothbrush and the cat and been gone at the first eerie sound.

There it was again. A chilling sound that echoed around the big hall. Mrs O'Dea flung open the library door and switched on the light. Nothing. Just shelf after shelf of books. Jack was shaking his head.

'Same old thing,' he said. 'Once we get to where the voices are coming from, they stop. Wait until you see, it will be the drawing-room now. Or else the back stairs.'

We stood still, not quite knowing what to do next. I scanned the room, hoping for some movement, someone hiding somewhere. I was working very hard at convincing myself that those voices belonged to people with flesh on their bones.

But there was just an eerie silence. Jamie raced up a metal staircase that led to a gallery which ran around three sides of the room. He looked down at us and spread his hands in a negative gesture.

'Nobody up here,' he said.

As soon as he'd said it, the laughter broke out again. The same childish laughter, like a stuck record.

'The drawing-room!' said Mrs O'Dea.

Once more we raced after her, bursting into the drawing-room which was the next door up the hall. Again there was no sign of activity. This was seriously scary stuff.

'Ssshh,' whispered Mrs O'Dea. 'Listen.'

We froze again. This time the laughter was more muffled.

'The back stairs,' said Jack.

And again we trooped to where the sound had come from. I needed to wipe my nose. But I couldn't because one hand was clutching Leo's sweater, the other was holding Jamie's. The back stairs was down the hall from the library. It was enclosed inside a sort of wooden partition, as if to pretend that it wasn't really there. Probably to keep people of the serving class out of sight of the gentry, I thought.

Jamie and David raced up the stairs. I followed more slowly. If anything was going to confront us, let them deal with it first.

It was dark and stuffy on that stairs-in-a-cupboard. Something flashed into my senses and made me think of my da. I couldn't imagine why; it's not as if he's Arnold Schwarznegger or some other tough hero who we could have done with right now.

All this chasing about went on for about an hour. Then everything went quiet.

'One o'clock,' said Jack. 'As usual.'

Now that we'd stopped, the screaming hab-dabs hit me sooner than I'd expected.

'This is mad,' I said, as I flopped into a chair. 'There's nothing human about this. Jack is right. This house is haunted.'

'Hold on, Maeve,' said Jamie. 'We don't know that.'

'For goodness sake!' I went on. 'What more proof do you need? We followed those voices from room to room, but there was never a trace of human entry. I'm telling you, it's haunted.' I couldn't believe I was sitting in a big Georgian kitchen at one in the morning having a discussion about ghostly sounds. Me, whose heart turns to melted lard if a curtain so much as flaps in my bedroom. 'I'm scared stiff,' I went on, giving an involuntary shiver. 'I couldn't stick it here even with a whole bunch of people. Jack, I just don't know how you can stay on your own.'

The old man was nodding. 'Perhaps you're right,' he said. He looked across at Mrs O'Dea. 'Perhaps it has taken a fresh, young voice to make me see that my stupid pride is going to drive me insane. What's the point in going through all of this just so that Tubbemore House will remain in the family until I go to meet my maker?'

Mrs O'Dea was putting out cups and plates, a ridiculously ordinary thing to be doing after we'd just been spook-chasing.

She pursed her lips. 'I still don't think it's anything to do with ghosts,' she sniffed. 'But I do agree that the place is too big for you. I think you'd be wise to let it go, Jack.'

What a pity, I thought, that Jack's lover got a stupid disease and died. If she'd been vaccinated she'd have lived and there would probably be gangs of children and grandchildren whooping it up, making the old house ring. Then a thought struck me, as thoughts do when you're a creative person.

'Maybe those voices are the voices of children who wanted to be born into this family, this house,' I said.

Everyone looked at me. *Oops, should have kept that beautifully spiritual thought private, Maeve.* 'I mean,' I blundered, 'spirits of babies who would have lived here if ...' I tapered off. I didn't want to let the old man know that Mrs O'Dea had been discussing his love life with us. Jack was peering at me, waiting for me to explain. But it's hard to find words when your foot is in your mouth. I looked helplessly at the boys. They were suppressing giggles, the prats.

'I know what you mean, dear,' said Mrs O'Dea kindly. 'You mean the spirits of the generations who have gone before.'

'Exactly,' I fibbed, and left it at that.

'I think it has stopped for the night, Mai,' said Jack. 'You're very kind, all of you, to come and help me through this. But I'll be all right now. You go on home to your beds, you must be very tired.'

Mrs O'Dea was shaking her head. 'Not at all,' she said. 'We wouldn't dream of leaving you on your own. We're stopping here.'

I reacted to that with mixed feelings. On the one hand I

was glad that I wouldn't be spending the rest of the night alone in my bedroom. But, on the other hand, I wanted to get as far away from this tomb of a house as soon as possible. And, on a third hand – if there was one – it would be a cosy thrill, sharing the night in the company of Jamie and David.

'So long as we all stay together,' I said, just in case anyone got the bright idea of using the myriad of bedrooms upstairs.

'Of course we'll stay together,' said Mrs O'Dea. 'There are plenty of cushions and blankets. Anyway, it's warmer here in the kitchen.'

Jack got up. 'Well,' he said, 'I'm used to this. I'll carry on to my own room, if you don't mind. Thanks again to all of you. It's nice to know that there are people on my side. However, I've decided that I'll sell. I've been refusing an offer for some time now, so it won't be a long drawn-out sale. We couldn't have this carry-on any longer.'

Nobody said anything to that, mainly because he was absolutely right. It was okay for the rest of us, we'd be back to normal living in the morning, but he'd have to continue on with this eeriness if he chose to stay.

We watched him as he shuffled out, a defeated old man whose family pride was finished. I wished there was something I could do. I wanted so badly for it to be people who were causing all this unpleasantness. Let them be caught and thrown in the slammer and the old man could stay in his home. But I shivered when another part of my brain flashed 'spooks' loud and clear.

'What will happen to Jack?' I asked Mrs O'Dea.

She was plumping up some cushions. 'Well, for ages now I've been trying to get him to sell out and come to me. I think it's ridiculous holding on to this big old house just because of a name. It's a fine house, he'll get a good price that will give him a comfortable life.'

'You mean ... live with you?' asked Leo. 'In the lodge?'

Mrs O'Dea laughed. 'That's right,' she said. 'Nice and cosy for the pair of us in our old age.'

'Do you mean get married?' I asked, alert to romance in the offing. Very wrinkly romance, admittedly, but romance nevertheless.

'Goodness no,' said Mrs O'Dea. 'Jack and me go back a long way. We like each other's company, but no strings attached. Besides, we're too old for all that wedding palaver. Can you see me in a white meringue shuffling down the aisle? Perish the thought! No, Jack and I are fine as we are. The only difference will be that I won't have to traipse up here to see him and to bring him his dinner.'

'You give him his dinner?' I asked.

Mrs O'Dea nodded. 'Every day. Two o'clock. Regular as clockwork.'

God, no wonder the poor old devil looked like death! It was a wonder his teeth hadn't melted from Mrs O'Dea's curries.

We chatted some more and then, one by one, gradually fell asleep. Except for me, of course. I was finding it very hard to breathe with my head under the blanket. But the alternative was to be exposed to any ghouls or gangsters that might wander in. Something about that back stairs was nagging me. Something that was trying to tell me that it might be people after all. It's very difficult to argue with yourself about ghouls and gangsters with your head stuck under a blanket and everyone around you deep in slumber. What was it about that back stairs? It just wouldn't come to me. If I hadn't fallen asleep eventually, my brain would have exploded.

9

A Discovery!

After breakfast, we all squashed into Mrs O'Dea's thrill-a-second jalopy and headed for town.

'Are you sure you want to do this, Jack?' she asked, taking her eyes off the road to turn towards Jack.

Jack nodded. 'It's the thing to do, Mai,' he replied. 'You've been at me long enought to do it. Are you the one who's having doubts now?'

Mrs O'Dea pursed her lips and tortured the gears. 'No,' she said. 'I never had any doubts about what you should do.'

'Well, then,' said Mr Jack. 'Let's get on with it.'

They dropped us off on Newbridge's main street, arranging to meet us at half-past twelve. We didn't much feel like wandering around. There was too much to talk about. We went to a different coffee shop and sat at an upstairs window overlooking the street.

'I wonder if he's doing the right thing,' said Leo.

'Of course he is,' said David. 'Spooky old dump. He's well out of it. I'd have gone ages ago if it was me.'

'But that's another thing,' I said, tasting the brown sugar, 'if the house is really – you know – haunted, then won't he be selling the ghosts as well?'

There was a scornful snort. 'Ghosts!' said Leo. 'Get real, Maeve.'

'He's right, Maeve,' put in Jamie. 'Ghosts don't exist. It has to be someone with a grudge, or someone who wants him out.'

'Well, they've succeeded,' said David. 'And I'm on

Maeve's side. I come from people who are very close to the land and to a spirit world. I know it sounds daft, but there are things that we don't understand. My mother told me stories about our people that make me believe that.'

'Well, you belong to *our* people too, don't forget,' said Leo. 'And that side of you should tell you that those voices were human.'

I was gobsmacked that David was siding with me. Flattered, but at the same time scared because I actually wanted to be convinced that the voices were human.

'Should we go and tell the gardai?' asked Leo.

Jamie fiddled with his teaspoon before answering. 'I don't think they'd believe us,' he said. 'If they think the old pair are in some geriatric fantasy of paranoia, then what chance would we have of convincing them? They might even suspect us, and we don't need that hassle.'

'Anyway,' said David, 'If they'd wanted us to back them up, they'd have suggested it themselves.'

'Maybe we should go anyway,' I said. 'And we could tell them about your threatening letters as well, David.'

David made a face. 'No,' he said. 'Those letters are just from some crank. Mum would hate a fuss. It might just draw attention to us. Best leave it alone, eh?'

'Then we're back to square one,' I sighed. 'Where do we go from here?'

There was no answer to that. I looked out of the window, marvelling at how life below was going on as normal.

'There's Mrs O'Dea,' said Leo, pointing with his teaspoon. Sure enough, she was standing across the street, deep in conversation with someone who looked familiar. When he turned his head I was surprised to see that it was Frank.

'Isn't that the estate agent bloke you're pally with, Maeve?' said Jamie, giving me a sly grin. 'The cultured dude who talks poetry?'

I could have thumped him for that. But I didn't, because the smarty-pants swots in his school wouldn't have done that and I wanted to be sophisticated.

'Maybe she's giving him some cookery tips,' I said.

We laughed at that. But as I laughed, the nagging memory of my conversation with Frank returned to bother me. The image of me and Frank on a Harley didn't fit in with the image of someone who wrote stupid letters. *Have sense, Maeve,* I told myself.

'I suppose he's handling the sale,' Jamie was saying.

That knocked us back to sobriety.

We met Mrs O'Dea and Jack at twelve-thirty as agreed. Mrs O'Dea suggested we all go for a bowl of soup to celebrate Jack's big decision. Celebrate? The old man didn't seem too celebratory to me. In fact his shoulders drooped more than ever and his shuffle was even shufflier. However, he put up a brave front. Even though it wasn't long since we'd had coffee, we slurped our way through the mushroom soup with gusto.

'So, the deed is done then, Jack?' said Jamie.

Jack nodded slowly. You could see that this was breaking his heart. And here we all were, pretending that it was a good day's work to have started wheels in motion to erase his Horton heritage. It didn't seem right.

'Are you glad?' I asked.

He gave a sigh before nodding slowly again. 'Apart from all this ... trouble,' he said. 'It's time to move out anyway. The house is too big for me. It needs people. It needs voices and laughter.'

'Well, it has voices all right,' I said quietly. 'That's what kills me. If someone is trying to frighten you out, then they've succeeded, haven't they?'

If Mrs O'Dea had laser eyes, she'd have cut me in two.

'Don't be saying that, Maeve,' she said evenly. 'Jack is right. Apart from all this nonsense, the house is too big. Anyway, you said yourself that you'd have packed up and gone if it was you.'

Well, that was true. Still, neither spooks nor human creeps had the right to bring this about. The more I thought about it, the more confused and frustrated I became. I couldn't find the right words to put forward my feelings.

'Is it final now?' asked Jamie. 'Have you signed the contract and all that?'

Jack sighed again. 'Soon,' he replied. 'Whenever the contract is ready for me to sign.'

'And ... that will be that, then?' said Jamie.

'That will be that,' echoed Jack. 'Once I've signed on the dotted line, the sale will go ahead.'

We all sank into an uncomfortable silence. The only one who seemed pleased was Mrs O'Dea.

'Think of the comfort, Jack,' she said softly. 'With all that money, you'll live in comfort for the rest of your life. You deserve that, man.'

Jack wiped his mouth with the hotel napkin and crumpled it among the crumbs on his bread plate. 'Money isn't of much concern to me, Mai,' he said. 'But I know what you mean.'

I'd quite forgotten about the money aspect. Of course he'd be worth a fortune. And he was going to live at the lodge with Mrs O'Dea ...

Edgar's house was about three miles from the lodge.

'Should we bring a present, d'ye think?' asked Leo, as

we set off. 'Before we pass the shop.'

'Are you joking?' I scoffed. 'Isn't it enough that the little twerps will have the pleasure of our gracious company? I'm not parting with any of my valuable dosh to buy some spoilt kid something he'll probably toss in the bin.'

'A card, then?' said Leo. 'We can't go with nothing.'

'Yes, we'll buy a card,' said Jamie. 'And you can give it, Leo.'

I screwed up my eyes at Jamie. Sometimes he's such a wimp. David just laughed and said a card would do fine, that it was a cheap route to getting party nosh. That was true. I grudgingly parted with my 20p share and let the three of them go in to pick the card while I minded the bikes. As I stood there, listening to the racket that some starlings were making on the shop roof, a car pulled up.

'Hello there.'

It was Edgar. 'Just on my way home,' he said. 'I've taken an hour or so off for this party. The joys of fatherhood,' he went on, with that false sense of proud martyrdom that a lot of parents go on with. 'I'd better get a move on before these kids wreck the place. See you later? You *are* coming, I hope?'

'Oh yes,' I said. 'The lads are getting a card. From the four of us,' I added, just to show I'd chipped in.

Edgar laughed. 'That Australian chap with you?' he asked. I nodded. 'Good,' he said. 'Any further developments in finding his roots?'

I shrugged. 'Don't know,' I said. 'Dan Donnelly seems to be the only lead so far.'

Edgar nodded and gave a wave. 'See you soon, then.'

'Who was that?' asked Jamie, as the three of them emerged from the shop.

'Edgar,' I replied. 'He was asking if David had made any further tracks into his family tree.'

David gave a bitter laugh. 'I don't think we'll be around long enough to search any further,' he said.

'What do you mean?' asked Jamie.

'Oh, these stupid letters,' went on David. 'Mum's fed up. She's going to phone the people who are in our house to say we're cutting short our stay in Ireland.'

'You're going home?' I said.

David made a grimace. 'Looks like,' he sighed.

Rats! Just when we were getting really friendly. That kind of tore a chunk out of the day.

We rode on in silence for a while. The graph for this holiday was certainly no straight line. Too many dips and slants and not enough ups. Would now be the time to voice my suspicions about Frank? Maybe not. It was so incredible they'd laugh me to shame.

We could hear the shouts of the party kids from the gate that led up the long avenue to Edgar's place. All boys, of course. About twelve eight-year-olds. Several mothers with antediluvian Laura Ashley dresses and sun-bed tans were setting out sausage rolls, technicolour drinks and frilly little buns with Smartie faces. Jellies wobbled disgustingly, like aliens in their death throes.

Edgar made a beeline for us. I couldn't think why he was so glad to see us. Maybe he was just relieved to get away from the *Stepford Wives* and the screaming kids.

'Jane is an interior designer,' he said proudly as he hauled us over to his wife.

'Hello,' she said, looking at the four of us with as much interest as you'd show a plate of cold spaghetti.

'Right, kids,' called out Edgar. 'These boys will organise a game of soccer for you.'

Well, that put me firmly in my place. There was no way I was going to suffer the indignity of scrambling about with a bunch of screeching kids. That left me with the Frocks. I should have stayed at home.

THE LONELY MAIDEN IN SOME SAD PART OF HISTORY

By Maeve Morris

She stood alone among the crowd
Of rabble-rousers, very loud.
The women watched, kept her in check,
Jealous of her youthful neck.
They sniggered at her lonesome face
As her men were dragged to another place.
'I will not be like you!' she cried.
And, lying down, she upped and died.

'Are you staying locally?' one of the women asked.

'Yes,' I replied. 'We're staying with the Montgomerys. At the dower house,' I added for good measure. A polite smile made its way around the surrounding faces. 'That's the nickname we have for the lodge,' I explained, just so that they wouldn't think I was totally dumb. And to show that I was part of an upmarket scene.

'Ah, you're with the Montgomerys?' another voice put in. 'How is Phyllis?'

'Phyllis?'

'Mrs Montgomery. Is she well?'

Now I was stumped. 'She's okay,' I replied. A safe enough answer. After all, it covered everything from being A1 healthwise through to severe leprosy.

'She got over her sprained ankle then?' asked Jane. 'She

sprained it at tennis last week,' she explained to the others. 'I had to help her to her car, poor dear.'

The others tut-tutted and Jane beamed, as if glad to be able to brag that Mrs Montgomery was indebted to her.

'Oh, the ankle?' I said. 'No, they're not happy with it at all. She shouldn't have put weight on it. They think she's going to lose the foot. Gangrene and all that. Can I use your loo?'

I smirked as I followed Jane's directions to the bathroom. Here at least I could lock myself away until the boys were available again.

After I'd tried the various handcreams and talcs in the bathroom and peered into the big airing cupboard, I wandered downstairs again. Halfway down I heard voices coming from the room that I'd already discovered was a study. The door was open.

'I photocopied those for you,' Edgar was saying. 'When someone mentioned the Dan Donnelly connection, I got my hands on some old cuttings and photocopied them for you. In fact, from what you've told me about your grandfather, I feel you could be on the right track. That's the funny thing about senile dementia, early memories become very lucid. My own grandfather used to talk about the first world war as if it was yesterday, but he scarcely mentioned it before he went senile. Anyway, it's something to go on, isn't it?'

'Sure. Thanks,' said David's voice. 'I'll show these to Mum.'

'They're only newspaper reports of Donnelly's fights,' went on Edgar. 'But they might come in useful. If I can be of any further help, tell your mum to contact me.'

Good old Edgar, I thought. Too decent to be married to an iced cod.

'Great,' said David.

I continued down the stairs, very loudly so that they wouldn't know I'd been listening.

'Ah, Maeve,' said Edgar. 'I've just been telling David here that he could be right in following up the Dan Donnelly link. Even though Donnelly wasn't born here, he fought here. David and his mother should concentrate on the Dublin connection. Dan Donnelly owned several pubs in Dublin.'

David held up the few tatty photocopies. I could see that he was making an effort to look enthusiastic. 'We'll read these, Mum and me,' he said.

I swallowed a snigger. I knew David didn't really give a toss about all this ancestry stuff. Not really. And especially not now, with all that had been happening.

'Let's get back to the game,' said Edgar. 'It's great that you boys can entertain these little horrors. I have to leave soon.'

Here we go again, I thought. Don't mind me. I'll just curl up and pretend I don't exist. As if!

'Can I have a look at your books?' I asked, thinking there might be something spicy among the dusty old books.

Edgar hesitated for just a nano second. Then he held out his hands in an agreeing gesture. For some reason he reminded me of a drag queen without his frock.

'Sure,' he said. 'Look away.'

Well, what else could he say? After all I'd given 20p towards his son's soppy birthday card.

David winked at me and followed Edgar from the room. Alone again! I was regretting more than ever that I'd come to this cruddy party. I should have known that we were asked for a reason. Nobody invites teenagers to a kids' party unless they want to make use of them. Well, I, as sure

as hell was not about to be made use of. The study would offer refuge and, at the same time, make me appear an intellectual.

I was drawn first to the desk – a big affair dominated by an Apple Mac and a fax. The screensaver was on. It showed toasters with wings flying about. I'm not normally one to pry – except when I'm very bored. This was a very bored time, so I shuffled the mouse to see what was on screen. It was a letter addressed to some international hotel group. Edgar had obviously been writing the letter just recently. I glanced quickly. It said: 'Dear Mortimer, Many thanks for your impressive brochures. Your hotels certainly stretch around the world. You'll be delighted to learn that we've reached a decision...'

I jumped when the fax ticked into action and a message began to come through. It was headed with the name of the same hotel group and it began: 'Delighted with your fax. All systems go then ...' Yeah, yeah. I didn't bother taking in any more because it was as boring as you'd expect from someone with the name Mortimer.

Lucky old Edgar, I thought, glancing at the classy brochures that were scattered on the desk. Obviously he and his family were heading off on holiday to one of these palatial hotbeds of pampering and posh nosh. No B&B or damp caravan for the Edgar clan. There was money to be made in sending people to the nick, or even keeping them out of it. I wondered, for just a second, if I might do a law degree so that I too could fax the Mortimers of this world to tell them I'd be coming for a holiday. But I figured there were too many words to read before you'd end up in a dusty old office in some dreary town. Besides, you'd have to mix with people of the criminal type who might do weird things if you lost their case. I'd stick with being a famous poet.

I switched my attention to the bookshelves. As I suspected, the books were dire. I'd die of boredom before this day was out, I thought. I looked at the higher shelves. Art books. There might be some naked people to increase my knowledge of human anatomy. I climbed the step-ladder and searched along the shelves. There was this Picasso bloke who hadn't a clue; his women had eyes on the wrong side of their faces and there were boobs where nobody I knew had boobs. Then there was this American called Jackson Pollock whose paintings looked like he'd thrown up all over the canvas. At this rate I could be a famous artist as well as a Nobel prizewinning poet.

Just as I was replacing the Pollock book, something else caught my eye. It was a book with a photo of some big mansion on the front. The sort of book that people leave on a coffee-table just to show visitors that they're cultured. Well, *Great Houses of Leinster*, would fill in a half-hour or so. When I saw, on the flyleaf, a decorated label with the words: *Ex Libris B. Horton, Tubbermore House*, I did a double take. Then I remembered that Mrs O'Dea had told us that Edgar was a close friend of Jack's, so it would figure that they'd lend one another books.

But when I turned to page fifty-eight, I nearly fell off the step-ladder. There, in all its former magnificence, was Tubbermore House. It was all I could do to stop myself from running outside, brandishing *Great House* and screaming, 'Look at what clever old me has found!' But better judgement prevailed. Judgement that told me to hold on and glean any information myself so that I could be the one to claim all the glory.

As I read, my blood ran cold. And when I saw a reproduction of the painting of the folly which Jack had hanging in his hall, my brain turned another somersault. Not because of the painting, but because the article named the artist. It was then that several things fell into place. I looked at the pictures over and over, and read the words over and over, just to try and convince myself that that my imagination was running on overload. I looked out of the pseudo-latticed bay window to try to think logically. The kids were laughing and screaming. And, in the middle of them was Frank. I'd been so engrossed I hadn't seen him arrive. My heart skipped a beat. Confused? Was I what! There were several things I wanted to ask him, but he was busy. He had a camcorder on his shoulder and he was recording the kids for posterity. Recording their mad football game and their childish laughter.

10

Doubts and Suspicions

I thought my head would burst before we could get away from this place.

'Let's go,' I said to Jamie. 'You've done your bit. See? They're all exhausted now. All they want to do is sit at the table and stuff their silly little faces.'

'What's your hurry?' asked Jamie. 'Anyway I fancy a bite to eat myself.'

'I've tasted everything,' I said. 'It's all crap. Typical kids' party stuff. Come on, we can buy chips on the way home.'

'Get lost,' put in Leo, his face flushed and his tee-shirt decorated with grass stains. 'We've earned our grub. You've probably been stuffing *your* silly face while we were entertaining those kids. It's our turn now.'

'I've been in the study, reading,' I hissed. 'There's something I have to tell you, but I can't tell you here.'

'Tell us what?' laughed Leo. 'That you found a *Noddy* book you could understand. Pass me one of those egg sambos.'

I looked at David to see if he'd support me, but he was busily munching a sausage roll. How could I get it across to them that what I had to say was of the utmost importance? Well, if it took high drama, then I was the woman for it. If my ancestral sisters-in-poetry could throw a mean swoon when it suited them, or when their corsets were too tight, then I could do it too.

'I feel faint,' I said, forearm to brow and eyelashes delicately fluttering. Leo stopped mid-munch, looked at me, snorted and went on eating.

'I'm not at all well,' I persisted. Then I launched a beautiful, elegant drop to the grass after making sure that there were no death-threatening toys or other hazards within swooning distance. And also making sure that the book I'd borrowed was well hidden under my loose sweatshirt. At first nobody noticed my swoon and I wondered if I should get up and do it again, but that would rather spoil the effect. Then I was conscious of voices around me. It was all I could do to keep my eyes closed.

'Maeve!' Jamie's voice. Good, he sounded concerned.

'Hey, mate!' That was David.

'Is something wrong?' Frank's voice, coming nearer.

'She's okay.' That was Leo.

Someone had taken up my beautifully limp hand. God, I was good at this. Then I felt a sharp pain under a fingernail which caused me to cry out and leap up. I could have exploded when I saw Leo grinning at me, and I could have thrown up when I realised it was he who'd held my hand.

'What do you think you're doing, you little prig,' I screeched.

'I knew it,' he grinned. 'You were putting on an act.'

'What do you mean I was "putting on an act"?' I muttered, sucking my injured finger.

'That's a trick I read about,' he gloated. 'If you think someone is pretending to faint, you shove your thumbnail behind one of their fingernails and press hard. If they don't leap up, then they've really fainted. But if they do jump up, just like you did, then they're spoofing. You're just a big spoofer, Maeve.'

I glowered at him, willing him a horrible death right there, right now. A slow death with disgusting, exploding boils and unbearable pain. The party kids thought the whole thing was staged for their entertainment and were whooping with laughter.

'Nice one, mate,' laughed David.

'I really felt ill,' I said, with as much dignity as I could muster, under the circumstances. Which didn't amount to much, unfortunately.

I jumped when I felt a hand on my shoulder. It was Frank. He looked at me with concern. 'Are you all right, Maeve?' he said.

Only a short while ago I would have thought I'd died and gone to heaven by having his gaze on me like this. But not right now.

'I'm all right,' I said, pushing his hand away.

He gave the boys a helpless look, shrugged his shoulders and went back to his filming. Jamie looked puzzled.

'What are you at, Maeve?' he said.

'Nothing,' I muttered. 'Can we go soon?'

'She's crazy,' said Leo, through a mouthful of sandwich.

'Oh dry up, Leo,' I said. 'I hope that egg is full of salmonella.'

Edgar's wife came over to me, more annoyed than concerned because here was something to mar her prissy party. 'Are you all right, dear?' she asked. 'Have you a little tummy-ache?' she added in an undertone. But not undertone enough. Out of the corner of my eye I could see Leo spluttering egg, and David and Jamie trying not to do the same. Let any of them ever mention this and I would have them screaming for an ambulance. Embarrassed? I wanted to die. Silly woman. Silly party. But, worst of all, silly me for bringing this whole scene together. It was my own silly fault. No backing out now.

'Thank you for asking,' I said. 'I think I'd better go home.'

'Well, if you're sure,' she said, hardly disguising the fact that she'd be glad to see the back of someone who had no useful purpose here.

Without a backward glance at any of them, I got on my bike and sailed down the avenue, my face burning with embarrassment and anger.

'What the devil kept you?' I asked, jumping off the low bridge where I'd been impatiently churning things over in my mind. 'I've been waiting here for ages. What were you at?'

The three boys looked at me in amazement.

'Oh no. It's the Bridge Troll,' groaned Leo. 'Got a little tummy-ache, Troll?'

I ignored his remark. There were more important things to talk about right now.

'We thought you'd really gone, Maeve,' said Jamie.

'Well, you took your time coming after me,' I said.

'What's wrong?' asked David. 'Why are you acting like this, Maeve?'

I looked at him and screwed up my eyes for added effect. 'Your ancestry thing,' I said. 'That's what's wrong.'

'What do you mean?' The way he asked made me wish I hadn't been so dramatic.

'What I mean is …' I swallowed to lubricate my dried-up throat. The enormity of what I had to say suddenly hit me. 'Look, could we find some place to sit. I don't want to stand here in case … in case someone comes along.'

'Maeve!' exclaimed Jamie. 'Just what are you playing at? For heaven's sake!'

'Told you,' muttered Leo. 'Crazy as a loon.'

But David was looking at me with a mixture of puzzlement and impatience.

'Trust me,' I said. 'Please.'

We dragged the bikes into a ditch and climbed through a hedge into a field.

'This will do,' I said, settling down on a clump of grass. The boys were still looking at me uncertainly. 'For goodness sake I'm not going to chop your cruddy heads off,' I exploded. 'Sit down.'

They were so dumbstruck, they sat down. For once the thrill of power passed me by. I fumbled under my sweatshirt and pulled out the book.

'What's that?' began Leo. 'Did you nick that?'

'Don't be stupid,' I said. 'I borrowed it. Anyway it belongs to Jack, I'll be simply returning his property. Look, it's about great houses in Leinster ...'

'Is that all?' interrupted Leo. 'All this ...'

'Let her finish, Leo,' said David, his eyes never leaving my face. I gulped. What if I was wrong? He'd be so angry. I couldn't bear that. I spread out the book at page fifty-eight. 'Listen,' I said. 'This is all about Tubbermore House. You remember that painting you were looking at in Jack's house? The one that he said was painted by his mother?' I added when I saw David's puzzled face.

'The one of the folly?' asked Jamie.

I nodded. 'That's the one. Well, here's a reproduction of that painting,' I went on. 'And the name of the artist was Emily Horton.'

'We know that,' scoffed Leo, peering over my shoulder. 'Jack's mother. He told us that himself. What's your point?'

'The point is,' I continued, 'that this Emily Horton's maiden name was Kelly.'

David shrugged. 'So?' he said. Darn his coolness, I thought. Why wasn't he jumping up and down like I expected him to do? 'There were thousands of Kellys. Like Leo says, what's your point?'

'Ah,' I replied. 'This is where it gets interesting. Tubbermore House was owned by the Kellys. Emily inherited it from her father. It's not a Horton estate, it's a Kelly estate, going right back to the seventeen hundreds.'

'Maeve,' Jamie put in gently. 'I can't see where this is getting us.'

'Oh, just listen,' I said impatiently. 'I was getting to the important bit. It says here that this Emily Horton had a brother who left home as a young man and never returned to claim his inheritance.'

David's eyes were still on me, making me feel uneasy. His jaw was set in that vaguely familiar way. 'His name,' he said evenly. 'What was the name of this brother?'

'Richard,' I said softly, stabbing the print with my finger. I crossed everything I could cross and prayed that this name would ring the bell. I knew I'd hit target when I saw David's face go as pale as coloured skin can go. 'Richard Kelly.'

David pursed his lips. 'My grandfather was Richard Kelly,' he said. Then he shook his head. 'Still, that's probably just coincidence ...'

'One of the Tubbermore Kelly ancestors was a man called Captain Kelly,' I went on, turning the page. 'He's the man who took Dan Donnelly under his wing. He's the one who organised his first fights and helped to make him famous. Captain Kelly and his brother had racing stables here in Kildare. That was back in the early eighteen hundreds. See? The Captain lived in a place called,' I paused to run my finger down the page, 'called Maddenstown. The other brother went into his own racing business and built Tubbermore House. *That's* the

Dan Donnelly connection. Your grandfather was talking ancient history when he went ga-ga, remembering bits of childhood stories. Old people do that. Dan Donnelly was probably a big folk hero for the Kellys, but he was no relation. You've been following the wrong trail.'

I hoped nobody would remember that it was me who'd got all excited about the Dan Donnelly bit. There was a silence, only broken by passing cars. A tense silence that you could cut with a lollipop stick. I looked at faces for a reaction. 'Oh, for heaven's sake!' I spluttered. 'Do I have to spell it out for you? The Tubbermore Kellys must be your ancestors. Are you deaf or blind or what?'

'I don't know,' began David. 'I can't take all this on board. I don't want to get my hopes up. It's all too far-fetched.'

'Far-fetched or not, it must be true,' I put in. 'You think I'm an eejit, don't you?'

I was getting annoyed now. Nobody had reacted in the positive way I'd expected. I was beginning to doubt myself. Jamie leaned across and tapped David's knee.

'Why don't we head back to Tubbermore and ask Jack?' he suggested. 'Maybe he can fill in the gaps.'

David shrugged and threw away the blade of grass he'd been fiddling with.

'Sounds okay to me,' he said. 'Just, let's not hold our breath, eh?'

I was about to say something scathing about the lack of gratitude, but Jamie cut across before words could leave my mouth.

'Come on, so,' he said, getting up and climbing through the hedge.

But the doubts and suspicions battled in my mind as I struggled through the hedge. What had I got myself into?

I was beginning to feel sorry that I'd ever set foot in this flat county with its mad story about a big cloak. Well, if people thought Brigid was mad, they'd sure as hell think I was dead crazy if my story proved to be wrong. I looked up to where heaven is supposed to be.

'Listen, O Saint Brigid of the Large Clothes,' I prayed. 'Gimme a hand here. Shuffle around up there and see if you can find an old ancestor to put us on the right track.'

I stuffed the book back inside my sweatshirt, mounted up and followed the boys.

Mrs O'Dea's dusty and dented car was parked at the steps when we got to Tubbermore House. She was in the kitchen and looked up, surprised to see us. The boys greeted her warmly. I hung back. I had my reasons, but I wasn't about to reveal them. One thing at a time, Maeve, my mind dictated.

'Party over then, is it?' she asked.

'Not really,' said Jamie. 'They're eating. And then I think there's a clown hired to come and entertain them.'

This clown has already given them their fill of entertainment, I thought ruefully. No clown would equal my performance of Lazarus rising from the dead. But of course I didn't say that. I was trying to put it way at the back of my mind, along with all the other personal disasters I wanted to forget.

'Where's Jack?'' I asked, looking around for the old man to toddle in and be delighted to see us.

'Gone,' replied Mrs O'Dea, sweeping the tiled floor with all the familiarity of a wife. Making herself useful and indispensable. Couldn't wait, could she, to get old Jack and his money installed under her roof. I could see it all now; slip the odd pinch of rat-poison into his grub – he'd never taste it over the gut-churning concoctions she made anyway – and, hey presto, he snuffs it, leaving her his fortune. The scheming old hag. I narrowed my eyes as I looked at her.

'Gone where?' I asked suspiciously.

THE SCHEMING OLD HAG

By Maeve Morris

Have a spoon of poisoned mash
And I'll inherit all your cash.
I've practised hard at cooking crap
To make you fall into my trap.
Folks will think me very kind
As I pretend it's you I mind.
I'll bury you with lots of tears.
And toast your bones with many beers.
But then I'll take the cash and run
To a land with sand and sun.

'Could be anywhere,' she replied, sweeping the dust on to the dustpan and emptying it into the Aga. 'I've just got here. The back door was locked, so he could be rambling through the fields. That's Jack, he just takes off.' She sighed softly. 'Probably having a look over the land before the sale. All this is breaking his heart, I know it.'

'You must be delighted,' I said, trying to keep the bitterness out of my voice.

'How do you mean, lass?' she asked.

'That he's selling,' I went on. 'And that he's moving in with you to the lodge. You'll have loads of dosh.' My anger had knocked the word subtlety right out of my vocabulary.

Mrs O'Dea looked up from sweeping the rest of the dust. 'Money is it?' she laughed. 'Are you thinking I'm after his money, is that it?'

'No, no, what she means is that Jack won't have any worries,' Jamie put in quickly. 'He'll be able to do anything he wants and won't have to worry about the upkeep of this place.'

It was a good attempt at smoothing over my gaffe, but it was dead lame. Mrs O'Dea sat down, still looking at me. She shook her head slowly. 'I know what you're thinking, all of you,' she said. 'You think I want Jack to move in with me so that I can control him and his fortune.'

'No,' Jamie and Leo said together. I shuffled my feet, and David said nothing. He was still in shock after my dredging up what I hoped was his history. Once more I was regretting getting involved.

'Listen to me,' went on Mrs O'Dea, leaning forward towards the four of us. 'Jack's money doesn't matter a toss to me. He can give it away as far as I'm concerned. I have enough of my own to keep me decent. My only concern is Jack. For years I've watched him struggle with this place, trying to make a go of it, and ending up selling sites for bungalows and leasing out the good land when the farming got too much for him. That man has paid the price over and over for his no-good uncle. Jack and I have a great affection for one another. It's none of your business, but Jack has asked me to marry him more times than I can remember.' She paused to take a wheezy breath, the brooch on her chest going up and down with the effort. 'Marry him and move in here with him,' she continued. 'But, no thanks, I've had enough of big old houses and, at our stage in life, marriage is just a bit of paper, not worth the bother. I'm snug in my lodge and it's there I'll stay. And Jack too, where I can look after him and we can both potter around for the time that's left to us.'

She stood up, hands on hips and cheeks quivering with anger. 'And you have the nerve to think that I'm only after his money!' she went on. 'How dare you! Get out, the lot of you. Go and slander someone else, but don't ever let me hear talk of this rubbish again. I thought you were a decent bunch of youngsters, I really did. Go now, before I ...'

'Mrs O'Dea, you have it all wrong,' Jamie went over and took her arm. 'Maeve didn't mean that. Sometimes things come out the wrong way.'

I had the good grace to nod apologetically. *Here we go again,* I thought. I was having a really bad day.

'Please, sit down,' Jamie said to Mrs O'Dea. 'We're in ... we're in a bit of a quandry over David and his ancestors. We were hoping you might be able to help us. Please.'

I had to admire the diplomatic way he was trying to swing the old lady round. She looked doubtful for a moment, then she let him ease her back into the chair.

'Well, I don't know how I can help,' she said grudgingly. 'Or even if I should listen to you. But go on anyway.'

Jamie turned and gave me a very meaningful look. The sort of look that you'd give someone who has just shot your toes off. A look that demanded a grovelling apology.

'I'm very sorry, Mrs O'Dea,' I muttered painfully. 'I didn't mean ...'

'Oh, stop tripping over yourself, you silly girl,' she said. 'Of course you meant it. Don't lie to me. I'm too old and too wise to be taken in. Go on,' she looked at Jamie. 'What is it you want to ask me?'

'It's about this house,' David put in, pulling up a chair and facing Mrs O'Dea. 'Can you tell us anything about the history of the house?'

'Why?' she looked suspiciously at David, then at Jamie.

'Mrs O'Dea, we think David might be connected,' said Leo, kneeling on the floor beside David's chair.

'It's just a vague idea,' went on David, almost apologetically. 'But Maeve found some stuff in a book that just might connect me to this house.'

Mrs O'Dea looked at David with amused amazement. 'You?' she said. 'But aren't you ...?'

'Part Aborigine, yes. But my mother's father was Irish. You know that.'

'And I thought you said that you might be related to Dan Donnelly,' said Mrs O'Dea. 'Why have you suddenly switched to this family? Hold on now, I'm beginning to smell some sort of rat here. First of all you accuse me of being after Jack's money. Now you're trying to say that you have a claim on the place? Come on, folks. Really!'

She gave a bitter laugh and made to get up.

'No! It's true,' I exclaimed, producing the book. 'It's all in here. This house was owned by Kellys since it was built in the seventeen hundreds.'

'That's right.' She looked up at me, not even bothering to ask where I'd got the book. 'Until Jack's mother, Emily Kelly, married a Horton just before she inherited the place. Everyone around here knows that. But that doesn't mean ...' she began, looking at David again.

'No, listen,' I drew into the circle and knelt down beside Leo. 'You must just listen.'

11

Searching for Spooks

And so we told her all we knew, pointing now and then to paragraphs in the book. Every so often she'd nod or shake her head. But when I'd finished, she sat in silence for a few moments.

'No, too far-fetched,' she said then. 'Couldn't be.'

'Why?' I asked.

She looked at me intently. I hoped she wasn't going to hold my big gaffe against me and order us out again. But she shook her head again. 'You say your grandfather's name was Richard?' she asked David. He nodded. 'And he never spoke about his Irish ancestry?' David nodded again. Mrs O'Dea gave a great sigh and pursed her lips. 'Yes, there was a Richard,' she said. 'He was Emily's brother. He was born in 1907, four years after his sister. My own mother remembered him. She said he was a fine, handsome fellow. The son and heir, his parents doted on him. He was spoiled rotten. It was intended that he would follow the family business of breeding and training horses. And it seemed like he would. He was brilliant with the horses. It was said that he could even ride them bareback, he had such control.'

There was an exclamation from Leo. 'Just like ...!' He looked up at David, whose jaw was set in that same expression as when he'd been asking me questions just a short while ago.

'Sshhh,' said Jamie. 'Go on, Mrs O'Dea.'

'Well, Richard fell in with a bad lot,' she went on. 'To cut a long story short, he got deeper and deeper into gambling. He was rich and gullible and soon fell foul of older smart alecs who were quick to relieve him of his cash. It wasn't long before he had gambling debts that ran into thousands. The parents were devastated. But the honour of the family was at stake, so his father paid the debts. According to staff at the time, there was a terrible row. Richard stormed out, like the spoiled wretch he was.'

I stole a glance at David to see how he was taking on board the notion that his might-be-grandfather was a spoiled wretch. He was as po-faced as ever.

'Said he wanted nothing more from his family,' Mrs O'Dea continued. 'Said that he would make his own fortune. And that was the last they saw of him. The father died a couple of years later, they say from a broken heart, but it was probably illness. You know how people like to fuel bad news.'

'And what happened to the place?' asked Jamie.

'Emily and her mother tried to make a go of it, but they hadn't the feel for the business. Then Emily married Benedict Horton.'

'The "B. Horton" on the *Ex Libris* label,' I put in.

Mrs O'Dea nodded. 'He kept it struggling as best he could. But by the time Jack inherited, everything had more or less fizzled to this.'

'Oh, no,' I gasped. I just hate sad stories. 'Did he never come back, the brother?'

Mrs O'Dea shook her head. 'This is where it gets interesting. It was rumoured that he went to Australia.'

That made us all gasp. The jigsaw I'd spilled out seemed to be coming together. David went that funny colour again, his jaw set even more prominently. And then I remembered where I'd seen a jaw set like that before. The photos we'd been looking at that night of the spooks – the photo of Jack! I could barely keep back my excitement. But Jamie interrupted before I could get the words out.

'Just a rumour?' he said.

Mrs O'Dea looked at the backs of her hands as if searching for the right answer.

'Well, slightly more than that,' she replied. 'In the fifties, when times were hard, a local chap, Jim Buckley, went out on an assisted passage to find work in Australia. He heard about this sheep farm that was run by an eccentric Irishman whose name was Richard Kelly. He tried to find the place, but only got as far as the nearest town. In a bar there they told him that he hadn't a hope of getting an interview with Kelly, never mind a job. But someone there, who had worked at the farm, said that Kelly came from an important racing family in County Kildare. That he'd had a row with his family and hadn't been in touch with them since. I remember reading the letter myself,' she went on. 'This workman told Jim Buckley that Kelly had tried to build some sort of a tower but, in a fit of frustration, knocked it down.'

There was an exclamation from David. 'The *wamba*!' he cried.

'What?'

'The *wamba*!' Now his face became animated 'The ruined *wamba*. Grandpa Kelly used to show it to me.' He swallowed so hard that I could see his throat go up and down. 'I remember his very words. He used to point to the rubble and say to me, "Davey, that's a *wamba*, a monument to foolishness. Just as well it ended in ruins. And just you remember, lad, don't let any folly destroy your life." I never knew what he meant by that. How could a pile of stones destroy my life? It got that I was dead scared of that pile of stones. Then Mum told me that it had something to do with part of Grandpa Kelly's home and not to ask any questions about it because he never talked about his past.'

We were looking at him with puzzlement. He laughed. 'Don't you see?' he said. '*Wamba* is an Aboriginal word for something useless, something stupid. A folly.'

Wow! What could we say to that?

Mrs O'Dea was looking at David as if she was seeing him for the first time.

'Same high forehead,' she said in a low voice. Then she turned his head and studied his profile. 'Same stubborn Kelly jaw,' she went on.

'I saw that too!' I exclaimed. 'He's just like Jack's photo. The one we were looking at the other night.'

Mrs O'Dea shook her head. 'Maybe I'm just being fanciful after all you've told me,' she said. 'It's too far-fetched. It really is. I wish Jack was here. He could fill in the gaps. And yet ...' she looked doubtful again. 'And yet I don't want to get his hopes up. Just once he mentioned to me the uncle he never knew, but other than that he'd never mention him, so neither did I. And now all this.' She gave a sigh that made her cheeks wobble again. 'I wouldn't want him getting excited and then find ...' She paused again.

'... and find that it all came to nothing,' finished Leo.

She nodded. 'And for your sake too, David,' she went on. 'I'd hate to see you and your mother let down. I know she's anxious to find her Irish connections, but ...' She fiddled with a loose button on her cardigan for a few moments. Then she looked up. 'Especially with what Jack's going through right now,' she went on. 'What with the selling of the place and those voices.'

'Voices!' I said. 'Ha! I have a hunch about those voices. Trust me,' I added as the others looked at me with scepticism. No point in revealing my suspicions about Frank just yet; that might just make everything we'd been discussing topple into total disbelief. Tread warily, Maeve.

'I bet there's a passage behind these walls,' I said, getting up. 'I bet we'll find our spooks. Old houses like this used to have hiding-places for priests during penal times.'

'Oh, Maeve,' began Jamie.

Leo made a big show of burying his face in his hands. And David? Well, he had so much going on in his head that he just shrugged. It was Mrs O'Dea who rallied to my call.

'She could be right,' she said, making me blush with extra guilt over my crude accusation earlier. 'In daylight we might uncover the cause of all this hoo-ha.'

She's a game old bird, I thought. Like me, she could be swayed to believe in spooks or not, but, like me, she was willing to chance finding out. Maybe she was right, that time in the cafe, when she said I reminded her of herself at my age. And maybe that was why she hadn't come down on me too heavily for my motor-mouth accusations.

Stirred up by the excitement of it all, we set about tapping walls. First of all we tried the drawing-room, then the library.

'We should have done all this the other night,' said David.

'Too scary at night,' said Leo.

'The back stairs,' I put in. 'It has to be the back stairs. Mrs O'Dea, is there a torch?'

'You seem very sure about this, Maeve,' said David.

'I am,' I replied. 'I'm pretty sure we'll find our voices behind the walls.'

Mrs O'Dea returned from the kitchen with a torch. We all trooped to the back stairs. Whatever had stirred my brain cells the first time I'd come here, was no longer evident. It was just a musty old stairs behind a partition. We tapped and hammered.

'This is madness,' said Mrs O'Dea. 'I don't know why we're doing this. It's crazy. The whole thing is crazy.'

'Maybe,' I said. 'But we must see it through.'

'No,' she continued. 'The whole story you've told me. It's too strange ...'

'Hold it!' exclaimed Leo. 'Listen.'

We stopped. He was tapping at a panel halfway up the stairs. It was giving a hollow sound. We felt all around for some sort of switch, but there was nothing.

'It's only thin board,' said Jamie, shining the light towards Mrs O'Dea. 'We could break through, no problem.'

She hesitated for a moment. 'Oh, we've come this far,' she said. 'Go on then. See if you can get through. There's a sledge-hammer in the scullery off the kitchen. I just can't believe I'm doing this.'

Leo was off like a shot to fetch it. Jamie took it from him, hesitated, and then handed it to David. 'I think you should be the one,' he said.

David gave a twisted grin. 'Thanks, mate,' he said.

It only took a couple of swings and a lot of splintered wood to reveal the opening.

'It looks like there was an older doorway here originally,' said Jamie. 'See? You can see where the original panelling was.' He ran his hand along the sides of the opening.

Mrs O'Dea had her hands to her mouth.

'Dear, oh dear,' she muttered. 'What do I tell Jack if all this is for nothing?'

'Tell him we were looking for mice,' I said. 'Big mice with boots.'

That sort of relieved the tension. Leo poked his head through. Jamie handed him the torch.

'There's another passage,' Leo's voice sounded muffled. 'It seems to lead to a door.'

'Wait,' said Jamie. 'We're coming through.'

One by one we climbed through the narrow opening. Mrs O'Dea stuck her head through last of all. 'Are you coming too?' I asked.

She looked at me with disdain. 'Do you honestly think I'm going to opt out now, lass?' she said. 'Make this hole bigger, someone. Let the old woman through.'

Leo was fumbling at the door ahead. Jamie shone the torch around the narrow passage. 'Dead clever,' he said. 'Who would ever suspect there was a hidden place behind those old panels?'

'Well, that was the general idea,' I replied. 'In penal times the English soldiers would shoot priests and anyone who hid them. Mass was forbidden, so everyone wanted Mass. That's how we Irish are – totally crooked. If we were invaded tomorrow and Mass was banned again, everyone in Ireland would be packing the churches and spouting Irish.'

Mrs O'Dea laughed behind me. 'You could be right,' she said.

Of course it was only then I realised I'd stirred up old history, the sort that had sparked The Row with Jamie. I looked ahead to see how he was reacting, but I couldn't tell much from the back of his head. Before I could say anything to try to make light of my remark, Leo let out a cry.

'There's a handle on the door!' he said. 'And it turns!'

There was a draught of musty air as the door swung open. We trooped through and found ourselves in a small chamber. Leo, once again hopping about like a mad flea, was stooping down, his face pressed against the wall. When he turned we could see a narrow beam of light coming through a small hole.

'It's the library,' he said. 'Look, you can see out into the library.'

We took turns peeking through. Sure enough, the hole looked right out into the library, facing the door.

'Aha,' said David. 'Shine the light up here, Jamie.'

Jamie shone the torch in the direction David suggested. There, nailed to the wall, was a small speaker.

'The first spooky voice,' said David. 'Follow the wiring.'

With him leading the way, we went further into the chamber and came out into another narrow passage. This one led to a small room with a spyhole overlooking the drawing-room. Again there was a speaker attached to the wall. And underneath was a ghetto blaster which was plugged into a time switch attached to the house wires.

'Meet the ghost of Tubbermore House,' said David. 'A tape recorder attached to separate speakers – I bet we'll find the other one above the back stairs – cleverly timed to come on at a certain time each night.'

'My goodness,' whispered Mrs O'Dea, over and over. Then she turned. 'Don't touch anything,' she went on. 'I'm going to ring the gardai. They'll take fingerprints. I'll be back in a few minutes.'

We listened as she struggled through the opening, and breathed a sigh of relief. Now everything would get sorted.

'But who did all this?' asked Leo. 'Who'd want to scare poor old Jack?'

'Haven't you worked it out?' I said. 'It's *Frank*. He's an estate agent, for heaven's sake. He'd have the sale of the house. He must have a client who's going to pay megabucks. *He's* the one who recorded those kids. Didn't you see him at the party? Prancing about with his camcorder.'

Realisation registered on the faces around me.

'The camcorder,' said Leo. 'It records voices as well!'

'Oh, Maeve, don't go accusing people again,' said Jamie. 'We don't know for sure.'

'Oh, suit yourself,' I said, with a toss of my head. 'I *thought* I was helping. Seems I was wrong.'

'Maeve,' said David. 'If it wasn't for you I wouldn't have found out all this stuff about my grandfather. If all this turns out right, I'll owe it to you.'

'And if it doesn't turn out right, you'll be to blame,' added Leo.

'Cool it, Leo,' said Jamie. 'If nothing comes of it, David won't be any worse off.

Two boys defending me. Suddenly I didn't feel such a low-life after all.

There was a shuffling sound and Mrs O'Dea's voice came from the outer passage.

'I'll strangle Jack,' she was panting. 'I've told him umpteen times.'

'Told him what?' asked David, helping her through the rest of the way.

'I've told him to pay his phone bill. Since he got the mobile he never bothers with the house phone, with the result that he leaves the bills unpaid and then gets cut off. I can't get in touch with either him or the gardai.'

'And still no sign of him?' asked Jamie.

'No,' replied Mrs O'Dea, waving a scrap of paper. 'This note was beside the dead phone. I hadn't seen it until now. It says that Edgar picked him up on his way back from the children's party.'

'Well, that's all right then,' I said. 'At least he's not with that crook, Frank, who can't wait to get his hands on this property.'

'What are you talking about?' Mrs O'Dea's voice was shaking with emotion. 'You don't know? It's not Frank who's looking after the sale of the house, it's *Edgar*. Jack is selling direct to Edgar. Edgar is the buyer.'

Edgar! It was then I remembered just what it had been that stirred up my mind that spooky night.

12

To Catch a Thief

'The tobacco!' I exclaimed.

'What?' Puzzled faces turned towards me in the gloom.

'That night on the back stairs,' I went on. 'You remember I told you I had a feeling about it?'

Jamie nodded, the others just continued to gape.

'Reminded me of my dad. It was the smell of tobacco. Edgar smokes the same brand of tobacco as my dad. It was Edgar who'd been here!'

'No! Edgar is a friend of Jack's,' put in Mrs O'Dea. Then her face went floppy as her mind put things together. 'He came to investigate the voices ...'

I was nodding furiously. 'Go on.'

'He even brought the gardai,' she continued.

'And of course nothing happened,' said Jamie. 'Because he'd switched off the recordings.'

'I even asked Frank about it when I met him this morning,' Mrs O'Dea went on, still bewildered. 'I couldn't understand why it was to Edgar that Jack had gone, not to Frank – after all Frank is an estate agent. Frank said he was just as puzzled as I was. He said he'd no idea that Edgar was interested in the property.' She paused for breath. 'And now Edgar has picked up Jack. All will be signed and there will be nothing anyone can do about it.'

'And Edgar's a solicitor, which makes it extra legal,' I said. And then I remembered something else. 'That fax,' I said. Everything was tumbling so fast that my mind couldn't keep up. I tried to get all the words out before they could get mixed up and make no sense.

'What?' asked Jamie.

I took a deep breath so as to hold on to the information that was being signalled from the overloaded brain. 'While I was nosing around Edgar's place that time you were all playing football ...'

'Yes?' said Jamie impatiently.

'Well there was this letter on his screen addressed to a big international hotel company. I didn't want to be too nosy ...' I stopped to glare at Leo who'd snorted rudely.

'I didn't want to be too nosy,' I continued. 'So I just got the first bit where Edgar wrote that "the decision was made". Then I glanced at the fax and there was a reply to that saying how delighted they were that "the decision was made", and that now it was "all systems go".'

'The decision to sell,' said Jamie. 'Edgar must have faxed them to say that he was in a position to sell the house. He was going to do a quick deal with Jack and then sell on to the hotel company. They probably think he already owns the place.'

I nodded. 'And there was me thinking that he was just booking a holiday. There were all these brochures on the desk.'

'Oh my God!' whispered Mrs O'Dea. 'That explains everything. The pair of them will buy this shabby place for a song and sell it on for three times what they'll pay for it. No wonder they wanted Jack out. I still can't believe it. Edgar has been so good to Jack.'

'Huh. Big deal,' muttered David. 'Nursing a friendship just to bleed the old man dry.'

'What are we doing here?' said Leo. 'Why don't we stop them?'

'We're probably too late,' said Mrs O'Dea, with a gesture of hopelessness.

'Come on, we have to try,' said Jamie, leading the way back through the passage.

We trudged after him. I swore loudly when my jeans got caught on a rusty nail. As I pulled away, a chunk of denim tore away, plus a chunk of my knee. However, this wasn't a time for martyrdom, so I just swallowed my pain and soldiered on. We piled into Mrs O'Dea's car. She turned the key in the ignition. Nothing. Again she tried, and again no reaction.

'Come on!' I cried. 'We'll never make it. The house will be signed away!'

Mrs O'Dea looked defeated. 'Battery's dead,' she said.

There was a loud groan from the back. Then, in a flash, Jamie was out of the car.

'Come on, lads, help me push,' he said.

Mrs O'Dea put the car in second gear and let it gather momentuum. Then she released the clutch. There was a brief chug, a lurch, then full stop. She leaned out and shouted back to the boys, 'It's no use. Darn thing has given up the ghost.'

'Oh no!' I moaned. 'Now we'll never get there.'

'The bikes!' shouted Jamie. 'Come on.'

We followed him back along the avenue to where we'd parked our bikes. Mrs O'Dea trailed after us. As we mounted up, Jamie looked at her.

'You can ride crossbar if you like,' he said. You could see the relief on his face when she declined.

'I'd like to live for another few years,' she said with a chuckle. 'Go on, you people. Just be careful.'

Like a troop of Hell's Angels we sped down the avenue.

'Do you think we'll make it?' I shouted to Jamie who was way ahead.

'No,' he replied. 'But we'll do our best.'

'At the very least we can give those crooks a hard time,' put in David as we trooped out through the wrought-iron gates. 'Why go to all that trouble? What was the rush? He'd probably have got round the old man to sell eventually without doing all that weird stuff.'

'I think I know,' said Jamie. 'When did those voices start, can anyone remember?'

'According to Mrs O'Dea, about ten days ago,' said David, neatly avoiding a pot-hole.

'Aha! And when did you arrive?' asked Jamie.

'You mean ...?' began Leo.

'He wanted the sale completed before David and his mother found out about their ancestors,' I gasped, almost swerving into Leo. 'No wonder he kept going on about Dan Donnelly.'

'Delaying tactics,' said Jamie. 'To put them off the scent.'

'Never!' said David. 'I find that hard to believe. Anyway, how would he have known? We didn't even know ourselves that there might be a connection between Jack and Mum and me.'

Now was not a good time to confess that I'd been the one to spill the beans about David and his mother to Frank that night at the dinner. It was all I could do to steer the bike when the consequences of that simple conversation hit me. I wondered if there was an operation one could have to slow down one's mouth.

'Edgar's a solicitor,' Jamie was saying, his voice whipped up by the wind. 'Solicitors can have family records going back for years and years. Deeds, maps, details about the house – priest's chamber and all that. And he'd have known about Richard in Australia. Mrs O'Dea said that was common knowledge. He put two and two together.'

'That doesn't explain how he knew about my grandmother being killed by a horse,' said David.

'That I don't know,' admitted Jamie.

There was no holding off any longer. I had to get it off my chest before it burnt right through me, leaving me a smouldering mess here on the road.

'I think that might have been me,' I panted as I caught up with them. There, I'd said it – confessed. I kept looking straight ahead so that I wouldn't have to see the looks on their faces. 'That night at the dinner, I told Frank about you – because I thought it was a lovely story,' I added hastily, concentrating on the bushes that blurred into mottled greens as we cycled past.

'Oh, Maeve,' groaned Leo.

'Well, I was just being conversational,' I said defensively. 'How was I to know he'd use that information?' God, I felt miserable. Thank goodness we were moving fast enough for the wind to cool my burning face.

By now we were on the outskirts of the town, gasping for breath. Well, I was anyway. All this mad exercise was making my lungs, legs and heart think their final hour had come. With screeching brakes we drew up at the building where Jamie knew Edgar had his office. Two at a time we thundered up the stairs, past a dental surgery and an optician's, until we came a door with 'Edgar Jellett, Solicitor' written on the glass panel.

'That should read Edgar Jellett, Property Grabber,' I muttered, rubbing my aching legs. We took a deep breath as Jamie turned the handle. He pushed, then tried again.

'It's locked,' he announced. 'They're not here.'

'Are you sure?' I asked, pressing my face against the frosted glass. But all I could see was a distorted reception desk, which was also empty.

'Now what?' asked Leo.

'Who are you kids looking for?'

We looked up to see a man in a white coat. It didn't matter whether he was the eyeman or the tooth fairy so long as he might be able to tell us where Edgar the Shark and his nephew might be chomping their victim and spitting out the bones.

'We're looking for Edgar Jellett,' said Jamie.

The man frowned suspiciously, like some people do when they're confronted by a group of youngsters, as if we're all muggers and glue-sniffers.

'*Uncle* Edgar,' I put in. 'We're from the party. His kid's party,' I added. 'We've a message.' Too right we had a mesage for the prat.

'Ah,' the man looked relieved. 'He's your uncle then.' Nobody denied that. 'He's gone to dinner with a client.'

'Where?' asked Jamie impatiently.

The man shrugged. 'Couldn't say.' I knew by the way he said it that he was being cagey.

'Oh God,' groaned Leo.

The man looked concerned. 'I hope there's nothing wrong?' he said.

'Yes!' I put in before any of the other three could go all honest and say no. 'It's his wife. It's ... it's too awful. Fell down in a swoon, face like porridge, wheezing. Please, mister, have you any idea?'

He immediately changed his attitude. 'Something's happened to Jane? Hold on. I'm between patients – give me a minute and I'll drive you to the Ballymore Hotel,' he said. 'He usually takes clients there. Has someone called an ambulance? I'll tell my receptionist ... Hey, wait!'

We were already halfway down the stairs.

'That's just outside the town,' said Jamie, mounting up

again. As I pedalled after the boys I swore that, when this was over, I'd never ride another bike as long as I'd live. Anyway, who ever heard of a poet on a bike? None of the women poets on my list. But then, I don't suppose you'd do much swanning about on a bike when you have a tight corset and a couple of lungfuls of consumption.

We tore up the avenue to the hotel, past the shiny cars that were neatly parked.

'Ballymore means big town,' said Leo, giving us another chunk of the useless info that he often comes out with.

'Yeah, like we really need to know that, Leo,' I scoffed as we parked our bikes. But, for some reason, what he said stuck in my mind. I shook it away. I should know better than to even hear what he says. There were more important things to worry about – stopping Edgar and Frank getting their paws on Jack's house and David's heritage. Frank: I took a deep breath. Thank goodness I'd found out what a low life he was before I could reveal my deep and meaningful love. The unwritten poems about him evaporated there and then.

We dashed through the glass doors, making no sound on a carpet so deep you could die in it and never be found.

'Excuse me!' a strident voice rang out. We turned and looked at the reception desk where a woman with seriously flashy make-up rose to intercept us. The name Rita was stamped on a strip of plastic on her left boob. 'Where do you people think you're going?'

'To the dining-room,' replied Leo obligingly. He put his hands on the desk and peered up at the woman. 'We're ...we're meeting some people in the dining-room.'

'Oh no, you're not,' said rabid Rita. 'Not like that you're not going into the dining-room. Get your grimy paws off my desk, you brat. Out. All of you,' she glared.

We looked at one another and realised what she was on about. The four of us had the dust and debris from the secret passageway clinging to our clothes and hair. Not alone that, but my torn jeans and bloody knee were decidedly downbeat. Still, no one was going to call my cousin insulting names – except for me. I'm allowed. I put my arm around his shoulder protectively and gave him a reassuring squeeze.

'This boy has more brains in his kneecaps than you'll ever have. You're just a painted robot,' I snapped. 'Now, we have important business ...'

'Out!'

'You don't understand,' began Jamie, public-school attitude in full sail. 'We have to meet a man called Mr Edgar Jellett. He's a solicitor.'

'I know who Mr Jellett is,' retorted rabid Rita 'He comes here frequently.'

'Uncle Edgar,' I put in. It worked before, it might work again.

'I don't care if he's the grandaddy of you all,' she said. 'You're not going into our busy dining-room. I suggest you leave. Like now,' she added threateningly.

'Listen, Missus,' I made eye-to-eye contact, just to intimidate her, you understand. But it's hard to intimidate someone when your hair is full of cobwebs and your jeans are revealing your cut knee to the public. 'We've got to get to that bloody crook and his nephew before ...'

'Watch your mouth, kid,' she snapped. 'Now, get out before I call security.'

Jamie's shoulders sagged. 'Leave it, Maeve,' he groaned. 'We're probably too late anyway.'

'Not likely!' I exclaimed and, with a bound, I ran towards a sign that said 'Dining-Room'. As usual I'd be the one to save the day. Or so I thought. The hands that grabbed me seemed to come from nowhere and, before I could get my karate mode in operation, I was bundled outside.

'Big prat,' I muttered at the grinning heavy who closed the door after me.

The boys were reaching for their bikes. 'Nice one, Maeve,' said David.

'Nice one me eye!' I retorted. 'I was almost there when that gorilla nabbed me. I'm going to complain to the tourism people and have this hotel closed down for rough-handling their customers.'

In spite of the tension, the boys smiled.

'Never mind,' David said. 'Even with the house gone, we can still talk to Jack about my background. If it's true, then Mum and me won't have wasted ...'

'Look!' Leo interrupted him, pointing behind us. We turned to look. 'It's Mrs O'Dea. And your mum, David. Your mum is driving.'

Sure enough, a red car had pulled up and Mrs O'Dea was sprinting across the tarmac, David's mum close behind. We left down our bikes again and chased after them. There was no fear of them being stopped by the witch at the desk. We dashed in.

'I've told you lot!' spluttered Rita, little bits of spit sparkling in the sunlight.

'Mum!' shouted David. 'How did you know we were here?'

Eppie and Mrs O'Dea stopped in their tracks. 'We called to the office,' replied Eppie. 'We met a puzzled dentist who told us about a bunch of scruffy youngsters who were looking for Edgar. He directed us here. Now, come on. Mrs O'Dea told me enough to warrant our being here. These people are with us, dear,' she called to the now bug-eyed Rita, ushering us before her.

'Let's hope we're in time,' wheezed Mrs O'Dea, her heart probably gasping for a transplant

There weren't many diners in the dining-room at that hour of the evening. And there, over by a big window, we saw Jack and Edgar, heads together. Frank was leaning back with the air of someone enjoying an innocent meal. They all looked up with surprise when we dashed in.

'Don't sign anything, Jack!' cried Leo.

'What's all this?' exploded Edgar. 'What do you think you're doing, barging in like this? This is a business dinner. Mrs O'Dea, really ...'

'We're on to you, you scheming rat,' said Mrs O'Dea.

'Have you told Jack about the voices you planted? And the threatening letters to this lady here?' I added, looking directly at the man I'd once chalked up as a possible face to live with.

God, I prayed, *let me be right. If this turns out to be a cock-up, I'll never sing another Christmas carol, ever.*

'Let's not cause a scene,' said Eppie calmly. 'We're just going to sit and talk. Pull up some of those chairs there,' she said to us. 'And we'll discuss all this with dignity.'

She looked up at the waiter who'd come to investigate the interruption. 'A pot of tea for all of us,' she said, giving him a dazzling smile. I saw him shuffle off and shrug at the manager type who was hovering at the door. Boy, I wished I'd had her guts a few minutes ago; then no gorilla would have dared to throw me out.

'Jack, have you signed that thing?' asked Mrs O'Dea.

'I was just about to,' replied Jack. 'What's all this, Mai? What's going on?'

'That's what I'd like to know too,' said Frank.

'Yeah,' I said, with as much menace as I could muster up, considering how my machine-gun heart was ricochetting off my ribs. 'I'll bet you would.'

'I'll tell you what's going on,' Edgar put in. 'For some reason these people – these Australian people – think that they're related to you, Jack. They think they'll wheedle their way into your life and that you'll hold on to your house for them. Don't listen to them, Jack. I'm offering you more money than you've ever had in your life. Think of your comfort, man.'

'Excuse me,' I said, leaning towards Edgar. 'But what makes you think that Eppie and David think they're Jack's relations? We've never said anything about that to you. Mrs O'Dea is the only one we've spoken to about that.'

Mrs O'Dea nodded. 'She's absolutely right,' she said. 'We've only just worked all that out.'

There was an awkward silence, then Edgar became flustered. 'Somebody mentioned ...' he began. Then he looked at Frank. 'Frank told me things,' he went on. 'Things about this Australian lady's background ...'

Frank looked flabbergasted.

'Good act. He should get an Oscar,' I muttered to Leo.

'I did,' admitted Frank. 'I had no idea there were any deeper implications. I thought it a good story. What's all this about?'

'I didn't think you'd use that story I told you,' I said, narrowing my eyes at him. 'About David's grandpa marrying the woman he loved and her being killed by a horse ...' my voice tapered off.

'Hold on a sec,' Frank interrupted. 'I still don't know what's going on here.'

'Like I said,' muttered Edgar, 'these people have some daft notion about being part of the Kelly estate.'

Mrs O'Dea was shaking her head. 'You know that's not true, Edgar,' she said. 'You knew that a woman and her son had come from Australia to try to find their Irish roots – in a small community like this word gets around. That's what prompted you into scaring Jack.'

'How dare you ...!' began Edgar.

'Shut up,' Eppie cut across him. 'Go on, Mrs O'Dea.

'Got suspicious, didn't you? And looked up the Kelly records which have been in your firm since your father's time – only *you* could have worked out the truth. Then you panicked into doing the nastiest deeds anyone could imagine. Scaring Jack half to death and trying to get rid of his kin. You're a disgrace.'

'Now look here,' began Edgar, face at boiling point.

'All we told you, Mister Jellett, was the bit about Dan Donnelly,' I put in. 'Seems to me you were pushing that home to David back in your library. Putting him on the wrong track to play for time.' Not adding, of course, that it was I who'd more or less been pushing Dan Donnelly and his big hairy arms ever since I found that cruddy book which had cost me £2.50. Some things you keep to yourself and hope that others will have forgotten.

He gave me a squinty-eyed look. 'Watch your manners, young lady,' he said, glad to take the focus off himself and dump it on me.

'Let's not descend to rudeness,' said Eppie. 'We need to discuss this properly.'

We all stopped talking when the waiter came with a pot of tea and extra cups. I'd have preferred a glass of coke, but I had the good manners not to ask.

Edgar was flapping his hands about. Plump hands with ... Ha! Now I remembered why the vision of a drag queen had flashed into my mind back in the library; it was the red paint that had been – and still was – embedded in some of his fingernails. Like nail varnish.

'It was you who did the graffiti!' I exclaimed. 'The same paint is stuck to your nails.'

'What graffiti?' several people asked at once.

'That's right,' put in Leo. 'Maeve and I cleaned off some rotten graffiti so that David and his mother wouldn't see it.' Then Leo turned towards me, his eyes wide with amazement. 'Those letters and the graffiti,' he paused for breath, 'they started after the dinner party ...'

'After I'd told Frank about David's grandfather and all that,' I finished.

Frank slammed his hand on the table, making the crockery rattle. 'Look,' he said angrily. 'Will someone please tell me what's going on before I lose my mind. There are serious accusations flying around here and someone had better explain.'

Jamie and I swung around to look at him in amazement.

'You mean you don't know?' said Jamie.

Frank was looking at the red-faced Edgar who was struggling for words.

'Edgar?' Frank went on, 'you asked me here to witness the contract for the sale of Jack's house. Is there something I should know?'

My heart felt fit to burst. Was he really innocent of all these awful happenings? But before I could dwell on the turn-around , Mrs O'Dea leaned towards Edgar.

'You must have got a nasty shock when you realised that Jack's flesh and blood turned up out of the blue,' she said. 'Is it a hotel group you'd intended selling Tubbermore to, once you'd got your greasy hands on it?' she added.

Edgar stood up, face now an inferno. 'I don't have to listen to this,' he spluttered. 'I'll have the law on you lot for slanderous accusations.'

'Do that, sir,' put in Jamie. 'And we'll provide the tape of children's voices that you've been using. It will be interesting to compare those voices with the recording of your kid's party.'

With a growl, Edgar threw down his napkin and stormed away. Frank was shaking his head, as if he couldn't believe all this. Everyone started talking at once. Well, I was all talked out. 'Do you think Edgar doesn't want that dessert?' I asked. No point in letting an untouched meringue be dumped. I did have the good grace to offer it around before tucking in.

'Now,' said Jack, as Mrs O'Dea filled his cup. 'Will someone please tell me what this is all about?'

Epilogue

'It was Leo who drove home the final proof about your grandpa coming from here, David,' I said.

We were sitting on a wall overlooking the old stable yard behind Jack's place. Mrs O'Dea was inside with a joyful Jack and Eppie The evening sun was having a final peek at the day before shoving off to shine somewhere else. Probably Australia.

'How do you make that out?' Leo asked, amazed that I should be casting crumbs of praise in his direction.

'When you said that Ballymore means big town,' I went on. I could see Jamie smiling indulgently and shaking his head slowly, thinking I was going off on another wild tangent. 'You wouldn't understand, Jamie,' I said sweetly. 'But "*mor*" in Irish means "big".'

'And Bally means town,' said Jamie. 'Even a Brit like me knows that. So?'

'So what does tubber mean, if you're so smart?'

'A well!' Leo stole my dramatic lines. Ever since he went to the gaeltacht he has to jump in every time a blast of Irish comes up. 'It's spelt *t.o.b.a.r* in Irish. A well.'

'Exactly,' I said. ' And Tubbermore means Great Well.'

David was flabbergasted. 'Greatwell! That's where the name came from. So Grandpa Kelly didn't rub out his past altogether. He must have had some affection for the place if he called his Australian home after it. Jeez!' Greatwell, Tubbermore. Makes sense.'

'Everything makes sense now,' said Jamie. 'Your mother and Jack are still inside looking at old photos and chattering like ... like...'

'Like long lost relatives,' I put in.

'Weird, isn't it?' said David. 'I still can't believe I'm sitting here on land where Grandpa Kelly was born.'

'Little did you think when old Jack took a shot at us, that you'd find yourself heir to the estate,' said Jamie.

'You said it, mate,' laughed David, his earring sparkling in the sunlight. 'Come on, let's climb the hill so that we can have a better view.'

We jumped down, crossed to the front of the house and ambled up the hill to where we'd first set eyes on it.

'It's a smashing place,' I said. 'Dead romantic.' There was a snort from the other three. 'I mean it in a poetic way. But that's out of your league.'

'Oh no,' groaned Leo. 'Watch out, lads. Mrs Shakespeare is on the rampage.'

Pushing him on to the grass wasn't very dignified, I admit. But it was a laugh. Poets can't be thinking dreary stuff all the time.

'What's going to happen now, David?' I asked.

'Ha!' said David. 'What's going to happen is that I'm going to take Jack's shotgun and shoot intruders like you lot who trespass on *my* land.'

'No, seriously,' said Jamie. 'What will you and your mother do now?'

David rested his chin on his knees and gazed down at the house, its windows twinkling in the sunset.

'You know, the first time I saw this house I felt sort of drawn to it,' he said, neatly avoiding the question. 'Mum used to say that an Aborigine is spiritually drawn to certain places. I always thought that was baloney, but now I'm not so sure.'

I remembered how he'd sat gazing at it all right, that

morning when we'd first got to know each other. I'd thought he was just impressed by the big old house.

'And?' I prompted. 'What now?'

David picked at a blade of grass. 'I think Mum has already decided,' he said. 'She's talking of running a country guest house. She likes that kind of thing. Jack thinks that's a smashing idea. He says he'd help, that it would be a whole new life for him. They're like a couple of kids who've just found their presents from Santa. Mrs O'Dea said that she'd get involved too. She's talking practical stuff like tourism grants. She also says she could help with the cooking ...'

He broke off as Jamie, Leo and I let out a unanimous screech and fell about.

'Don't let her near the kitchen!' laughed Jamie.

'She'd have the guests screaming for mercy,' I added. 'But seriously, she used to be a housekeeper, so she could oversee the practical running of the place. And still live in her lodge.'

'This is Maeve, career-guidance bossyboots,' said Leo.

'Maeve is not a bossyboots,' said David. 'If it wasn't for her, Mum and me wouldn't have found Jack. And Jack would still think he was the last Kelly of Tubbermore.'

I felt a blush creep over my face. I hoped it was delicate pink, not lobster red.

'And she's absolutely right,' put in Jamie. 'That arrangement sounds good.'

The blush was now a raging fire, especially when Jamie smiled at me and winked.It was like one of those intimate glances that I'd read about in Mills and Boon. Tilly was right; playing off one bloke against the other really works. I had to admit I'd kind of cooled off on the Frank affair, even though he was totally innocent of all the grotty goings-on. Call it a fickle heart or whatever, but I think the hairy lip finally did it for me when I noticed a few grey hairs in it while we were all talking earlier on. That meant he was probably as old as Eppie. Now, there was a thought for a romantic sonnet sometime in the future, maybe. Meanwhile there were personal choices to be made.

THE TWO SUITORS

By Maeve Morris

They gazed at her, the suitors two.
Both loved her with a love so true.
Which will I choose? the Beauty thought
With heart a-thump and over-wrought.
They're both fine hunks, I love them so.
Oh deary me, I'm full of woe.
How can I break the heart of one
As by the other I am won?
Love can sometimes be the pits
Dividing romance into bits.
I know how Cleopatra felt
As beak-nosed Romans 'fore her knelt.

'And what about you?' I asked David, putting my hands to my face to quench the blaze.

David didn't answer for a moment. Then, 'I don't really know. It's all such a shock. I haven't really taken it in. Australia is my country, I don't know any other sort of life. Obviously Mum and I will go back to sort things out. She'll definitely come back as soon as she can.'

'And you?' I asked again.

David shrugged. 'Dunno. Maybe finish High School at home – Australia. Stay with my dad. Then we'll see.'

My heart sank. Just when things were getting interesting and I had mentally made arrangements to spend lazy summers here with people who would be only too happy to show their gratitude to me, David was stalling.

'Horses!' Leo announced.

'What?'

'He's right,' I said, pointing to the stables. 'You said you love horses. There's your chance. You could restore Tubbermore House to its former glory.'

David's face lit up. 'You could be right,' he laughed. 'It's certainly something to think about.'

I snorted impatiently. 'Oh, come on. Say you'll do it,' I said. 'And we could come and stay with you.'

David laughed. 'Okay, I'll definitely be back,' he said. 'One day I'll definitely be back to make those stables ring. You'll see. Tubbermore Stables. Me!'

There was the sound of laughter coming from below. Eppie, Jack and Mrs O'Dea were standing at the front door. When they saw us on the hill, they waved. They looked just right there on those Georgian steps in the evening light.

'Come on,' said Jamie. 'Let's go down and join the oldies.' He held out his hand to help me up. And I knew when I gripped it, that Jamie was the one I felt most comfortable with. Cleopatra had made her choice.

'Do you think I'm a fatal dame?' I asked him as we galloped down the hill.

Jamie stopped and looked at me. 'I think you mean a *femme fatale*,' he grinned. 'And yep, you are decidedly fatal, Maeve Morris. Deadly fatal.'

Well, that was good enough for me, whatever it meant.

MARY ARRIGAN lives in Roscrea, County Tipperary. As well as writing books for teenagers, she has written and illustrated books in Irish for younger children.

Her awards include the Sunday Times/CWA Short Story Award 1991; The Hennessy Award 1993; a Bisto Merit Award 1994; and International Youth Library choice for White Ravens 1997.

This is her fifth book for The Children's Press. The others are *Dead Monks and Shady Deals* (1995), *Landscape with Cracked Sheep* (1996), *Seascape with Barber's Harp* (1997), *The Spirits of the Bog* (1998).